DYING to FORGET

The Station – Volume 1

Trish Marie Dawson

Pretty Little Weeds
PUBLISHING

For Teresa.
Though you left us too soon, you will always be loved and never forgotten.
Your voice is always inside my head.

And for my family: Shane, Rory and Foxx...you are my loves.

DYING to FORGET

PROLOGUE

"Come on Piper, it's just *one* drink. Tomorrow's your birthday, after all."

"Okay, just one."

"That's a good girl."

Ryan nuzzles his mouth against my neck and everything inside me melts. I peek up at him through my curled lashes and see his bright blue eyes gazing into mine. The music is blaring around us; it's loud...concert loud, but I don't mind. The most gorgeous guy in the room is talking to me. Not to the perfect cheerleader girls decorating the packed room with their short skirts and tight tops and ridiculously perfect hair. *Me.* I give him a hesitant smile and he winks. I can't help the girlish giggle that escapes from my mouth and I feel my cheeks heat up.

I drink from the red plastic cup he firmly pushed into my hands, even though I don't like the taste of the bitter beer. Normally on a Friday night I'd be at home reading or watching Johnny Depp movies, but tonight was different. I had a date...an *actual* date. As he pulls gently on my fingers, I follow him through the crowd of celebrating seniors, weaving in and out of the jocks and preppy girls all in various stages of drunkenness. I watch Ryan's back as he walks gracefully in front of me. The contours of his muscles ripple deliciously below his football jersey as he moves around our classmates with determined ease. I want to reach out and touch his back but he has one of my hands in his and the other is carrying this stupid plastic cup, so I just stare. I barely notice we are going up the steps to the second floor until we reach the top and my gaze is pulled from Ryan's backside as he turns down the hallway, still tugging me behind him. *Where is he taking me?*

I almost think he heard my thoughts because he turns to look over his shoulder to smile at me. "It's quieter up here."

"Oh, okay." *He wants me all to himself!* I struggle to keep from jumping up and down with excitement and smile sweetly back at him instead. *Play it cool, Piper. Jeez.*

We pass two closed doors and one that must be the bathroom because there are several girls waiting outside it; flipping their long, shiny hair across their shoulders and glowering at me as I walk by with 'the' Ryan Burke. *They're jealous! Of me!* Something inside me laughs at them and I find it's not hard to keep my smile plastered to my face as I walk by. I take another sip of my beer, eager to finish the cup so I can put it down.

The room he picks is at the end of the hall and looks like it might be a guest bedroom. Once inside with the door closed, he flips on the switch and two bedside lamps flood the room with a soft yellow glow; warming the dark blue bedspread and casting deep shadows around us. A giant mirror hangs just above the headboard of the queen--size bed and it reflects the light well, but the room is still shrouded in a sort of romantic darkness. *What are we going to do in here?*

"Finish your drink, Piper," Ryan says gently to me while he closes the door behind him.

I sit down on the edge of the bed with my feet dangling several inches above the floor and sip from the cold cup. I still can't believe he's being so nice to me, so I smile and do as he says. After spending four years being ignored by the popular crowd, it's surreal being in a bedroom behind a closed door with the hottest guy in school. My stomach does a summersault when he sits down right next to me, casually resting his leg against mine. I can feel the heat from his thigh through my jeans. *Oh wow, he's beautiful.*

He starts talking about the game our team won the night before but I'm lost in the dark sea-color of his eyes and I find myself studying his face instead. He has large round eyes and long blonde lashes that match his thick hair. I gulp down the last of the nasty beer and ignore the fuzzy feeling in my head as I watch his mouth move. His lips curl up at the edges as he talks and when he laughs, my stomach clenches tightly. *I hope he wants to kiss me.*

"Are you done?" He asks.

"What? Oh, yes."

I hand him my empty cup and he leans across me to put it onto the small, wooden bedside table. He smells of soap; it's a very, very good smell. When he straightens up, he grazes my knee with his hand and I jump, my heart skipping at least a dozen beats. He grins up at me before leaning back on the bed, propped up on his elbows. After I copy his move and rest on my side, facing him, I think, *now what?*

"You have very beautiful eyes, Piper. I can never tell what color they really are…green, or brown, or blue. What color are they really?" His voice is like maple syrup; thick and sweet. *Yum.*

"Um…hazel." My voice is betraying me completely. It's as if I can't speak louder than a whisper with his face hovering just inches from mine.

Smiling nervously, I can't help but chew on the corner of my lip and notice that he's watching my mouth, so I very slowly lick my lower lip with the tip of my tongue. His eyes dart up to mine, surprised, I think. *He DOES want to kiss me!* I scream for joy inside my head.

Abruptly he sits upright, startling me. I push off the mattress slowly, unsure of what to expect. My head feels heavy and the room seems to tilt while I take a deep breath to steady myself. *Can one beer make you drunk?* I don't *think* it can and I glance nervously at my empty cup. I press my fists to my eyes, trying to rub away the sleepy sensation that I feel behind my lids.

And then his mouth is on mine. His warm, wet lips push against me as he pries my mouth open with his tongue. *Oh wow, I've never been kissed like this!* As I close my eyes, I get lost in the feeling and taste of him while he runs his hands up my arms, then my neck and into my hair. When he releases me his face is flushed; his eyes full of bright desire. *I can't believe Ryan Burke likes me!*

With trembling fingers, I reach up and touch the hard and chiseled contours of his chest while Ryan's large and strong hands roam over my entire body, feeling and squeezing everything. I've never been touched like this before and my insides are starting to freak out.

"I want you, Piper," he murmurs into my neck.

My mouth drops open in surprise and even though my brain seems to be telling me to jump and run out of the room, I'm unable to move, stuck firmly to the same place on the mattress. With my nerves on high alert, I glance at the door repeatedly, sure that someone will come bursting through it at any second but the steady thumping of the music downstairs reminds me that no one can hear what is happening in this room. No one cares that Ryan Burke took me, of all people, into a bedroom. That realization hits me suddenly. *Oh. My. God. What am I doing here?*

This is wrong. I don't feel okay, I feel sick. My head is hurting and I really want to get up and leave. The room starts to spin but what my brain and body seem to be suddenly disconnected, so I slump backwards against the bedspread and stare up at the ceiling. When I was a kid, the Tilt-A-Whirl used to make me feel like this...detached from my body just long enough to feel the world whizzing by. But this time the feeling doesn't go away.

The thumping of the music downstairs feels louder, vibrating through my body almost painfully. Ryan is somewhere close to me, cursing, and then he's hovering over my body, his blue eyes piercing into mine, looking through me. *I don't understand what's happening. What have you done to me?*

I can't fight him when he tugs off my jeans, throwing them onto the cream-colored Berber carpet like trash. My legs are heavy and useless and my arms are stuck above me and I realize too late that it's because *he's* holding them. Hot tears trickle over my temples, pooling into my ears. I try and scream *NO* but only a pathetic groan comes from my throat. *This can't be happening. Not to me.*

After he clamps one of his strong hands over my mouth, I look away from him and watch the door, waiting for someone - anyone - to throw it open and save me. I've made a mistake, a big mistake trusting Ryan Burke. Unable to get away from him, I close my watery eyes and hope that wherever my mind escapes to will be a better place.

I'm not aware of how much time has passed when Ryan climbs off the bed and scoops my jeans up off the floor, tossing them ungraciously onto the bedspread beside me.

"Thanks, baby," he says, slightly out of breath.

He smiles that gorgeous smile that now makes me want to punch him in the face hard enough to split his lip in half before he strolls from the room, leaving me whimpering. I'm broken in more ways than one. I don't think I'll ever trust another boy again. My heart fills with something heavy; I think it might be hatred. *My first time, this was my first time. How did this happen...to me?*

Trish Marie Dawson

CHAPTER 1

The wind blasts its way into the open window as we race down the road at breakneck speed. *Freedom, at last!* I ignore the trees that whiz by on the passenger side of the car and the yellow stoplight as I push harder into the gas pedal and fly through the intersection at seventy miles per hour. My heart pounds in my chest as Bree screeches loudly beside me.

"Slow down, Piper!" She hollers.

I ease my foot off the accelerator but don't tap the brakes yet. I glance at her and see her light brown hair whirling around her face and laugh as she braces her arms out in front of her.

"Oh, relax. I'm slowing down." I pout.

"Good, I don't want to die on graduation day, you know."

She laughs and visibly relaxes when I brake at the next intersection. While we sit at the red light I lean my elbow against the open window as Bree

9

launches into yet another lengthy story about her last date with her new boyfriend, Preston. I try not to seem too uninterested as her delicate hands wave the air as she goes on and on about dinner and the movie she doesn't even remember because she was too busy making out with Preston in the last row of the theater. *Yuck.*

When she finally pauses to take a breath, I push the radio button and on comes the crooning voice of Bruno Mars. Despite the competition to be heard over the music, Bree continues her story, boring me nearly to death. I itch absentmindedly at the bandage under my long sleeved shirt and push hard on the accelerator when the light turns green, lurching us forward. Bree sighs and I know she's glaring at me but I stare straight ahead, pretending to care about the traffic as we make our way through the irritatingly slow drivers.

"So, are you coming to the party tonight?" She asks in a perky sing-song voice.

"Um, no. Why would I?" I shift in my seat uncomfortably. Bree should know better than to ask me to another party.

"Come on, Piper! It's Grad-night! Don't you want to say goodbye to everyone?" She crosses her arms over her chest and blinks at me.

"I thought we already did that…today."

I don't look at her. She sighs loudly and eventually turns away to look out the window. I love her dearly but for some reason today she's just getting under my skin. I shift in my seat again and then turn the music up, hoping it's a distraction for both of us.

Five minutes later we pull up outside the roller-rink. Bree hops out of the car and sashays around to the driver's side, draping her slender yet perfectly curved figure across my door after I open it. Always the show stopper, she's wearing a short skirt with a new, body forming strapless top. All made of silk, no doubt.

"You know, I'm leaving in a week. I wish you'd come out tonight, just one last time. Please?" She looks at me with her big brown eyes, which usually make me laugh but there is no way. I'm not going to another party.

"Bree, I told you, I can't."

She huffs and waits for me to climb out of the car before slamming the door shut. I watch her open her mouth to say something else to me before her eyes dart to the side and her expression changes from frustration to one of pure happiness.

"Preston!" She squeals and rushes past me, into her boyfriend's open arms.

I nod at him and wait at the car for their impromptu make-out session to end. My arm itches again and I attempt to smooth my cotton sleeve over the bump where my cut is, cursing under my breath when I realize my shirt has gotten stuck to the bandage adhesive.

"You're hot, aren't you?" Bree asks at my shoulder.

"No, I'm fine." I smile at her but her frown deepens.

"Why'd you wear that shirt for your graduation? It's eighty degrees out here!"

"Bree, I'm fine, really." I laugh and playfully tug at the collar of her dress. "Are we going in, or what?" I ask as Preston sidles up beside her and wraps his arms around Bree's tiny waist. I squirm and try not to look uncomfortable.

"You're going to skate, right?" Preston asks.

"Um…" I hesitate just long enough for Bree to chastise me.

"Piper Willow, you said you would! You have to!"

"Uhg. Fine, let's go, before I jump back into the car and escape."

♡

As I lean against the carpeted wall with my sandals on the wooden bench in front of me, I watch couple after couple skate around the room, and the few stragglers that weave in and out of the crowd, hoping for a partner. Once we got inside Bree forgot completely about my promise to skate and disappeared with Preston. I saw her twirl around the room a few times and smiled at each of her friendly waves, but I made no move to join them. This wasn't my scene, not anymore.

"Wanna skate?" A boy from my English class interrupts my daydreaming as he slows to a stop and leans against the low wall that separates the seating area from the skating floor.

I shake my head a bit too fast and mumble, "No, thanks."

I don't bother to feel badly as his face falls and he shrugs before skating off into the mass of happy teenagers. Six months ago I would have jumped at the invitation. But now I almost hate boys. I have developed what Bree would label a 'cold shoulder' since what happened with Ryan. I doubt any guy will ever seem attractive to me again. Not now that I know what they are really capable of.

"Is this seat taken?"

Startled from my thoughts again, I jump at the sound of a familiar voice beside me and take a deep breath to calm myself before looking up into Ryan Burke's smiling blue eyes. *Bastard.*

"Yes." I practically spit the word out.

"Really, I don't see anyone around."

He gestures around me before raising his eyebrow, as if challenging me to argue. I glare at him before looking back into the crowd of skating teenagers, hoping to see Bree. I can't help but cringe as Ryan lowers himself onto the bench next to me and puts his feet up, lounging comfortably at my side, like we're best friends. I ignore him for as long as I can before the silence eats away at me.

"What do you want?" I snap, without looking at him. *Where are you Bree?*

"Oh, come on baby, why the hostility?"

He has the decency to look away briefly when I settle my icy gaze on his face. When he meets my eyes, he seems uncertain and for just a second - less threatening. Then he blinks and the old Ryan is back.

He stretches his long legs out before him and leans casually against the wall, looking me up and down. I snort with disgust as I remember how attractive I once thought he was. His hair is too thick, almost wiry, and his nose is crooked. I don't get what I ever saw in him. Now all I see is an ugly monster.

"You find something funny?" He lifts an eyebrow at me.

"Go away," I say angrily. *Damn Bree...where are you!?* My inner voice is loud and clear, *Get away from him!*

I stand up and turn to walk away, but Ryan hooks a finger into one of my back pockets, tugging on my shorts until I lose my balance and fall back into his lap. Waves of panic flood through my body as our skin makes contact and I scream, cutting off his laugh abruptly.

"Piper...*calm down!*" He says as he lifts me on his legs, his arms tightly around my waist.

People are watching now, but I don't care. I lift my hand and slap Ryan so hard across the face that my palm stings. He stares at me in wide-eyed shock, but surprises me by gripping both my arms and tugging me toward his face.

"I said *NO!*" I scream at him, feeling the now daily and familiar buildup of tears as they threaten to spill out of my eyes. This boy has turned me into a sobbing mess of a girl. And I hate him for it.

"You never said no to me, baby," he hisses.

His words are like a punch to the gut and I sit still for a moment, looking at him in a sort of stunned silence.

"Piper, are you okay?" Bree is behind us with Preston at her side and a handful of curious onlookers from the skating floor are staring at us.

Ryan releases my arms and I scramble off his lap in a flurry of ungraceful movements. My legs are shaking as I stomp away from him. I don't look back. I don't ever want to see Ryan's ugly face again.

The knife feels cool against my hot skin as I drag it up my forearm, watching tiny beads of blood spill out of me. The pain is an instant distraction and I sink deeper into the tub, letting the bubbly water splash over my shoulders and around my throat. When the water line is just below my chin, I pull my arm out to look at the small, clean cut I just made. It's still bleeding freely and I sigh, knowing I'll have to bandage it up before Dad gets home from work.

The paisley curtain above the tub shifts slightly as the breeze from outside the open window struggles to get into the house. The cool summer air feels good in contrast to the hot bath. I breathe in the subtle smell of lavender soap as the water cools around my body. I don't want to get out until my toes and fingers are pruned like raisins.

I don't move at first when my cell starts buzzing in my shorts on the floor beside the tub. I let it go to voicemail as I check out the new cut on my arm again. It's still bleeding. When my phone rings for the second time, I sit up with a sigh and reach down to pull the phone out of the back pocket. It's Bree.

"Bree, I'm taking a delicious hot bath. This better be good," I say in a fake chipper voice.

I bristle as I hear Bree sniffing back tears. "Piper, can you come get me?"

"What? What's wrong, where are you?" I am now standing in the soapy tub, reaching for a towel. Bit and pieces of the last party I went to flash through my memory.

"I'm at the party, remember? Preston's been drinking and he's being an ass, and…and, I don't want to call my parents. Can you come get me?" Bree is pleading with me.

"I'll be right there. Let me get dressed, okay?" I tuck the phone back into my shorts and slide my clothes on. My hair is still up in the messy bun I made for the bath and the lower half of my hair is wet, making the usual ash-blonde color a sort of chocolate brown.

I wave off my tired and makeup-less reflection in the bathroom mirror and pull my dark sweatshirt over my head, making a mental note to wrap my cut when I get back to the apartment.

I take the streets across town, speeding down the hills and rolling through stop-signs, hoping that Bree is okay. When I pull up in front of the party house, she is sitting near the curb, looking sad and tired, but her face lights up when she sees me.

"Piper! Thanks!" She says as she slides into the front passenger seat.

I lean over to hug her and give her a faint smile. She's wearing a new outfit…a skin-tight black dress with spaghetti straps and a pair of shiny red heels that look like they cost more than my car. Her parents must have updated her wardrobe for the summer. *How nice to be rich.*

It was obvious she had been crying since dark streaks of mascara covered her cheeks.

"Jeez, Bree…you look like crap," I say softly and she laughs.

"Let's go, before Preston knows I'm gone, please?" She asks and I oblige…pulling away from the curb with a screech of tires. We've gone half a block before she talks.

"Are you okay, I mean, after seeing Ryan today?" She asks quietly.

I glance away from the dark road to look at her. Her eyes glint in the pale moonlight and I can see the sparkle of her new diamond earrings. They were a graduation present from her parents.

"I'm fine." I force my voice to stay steady.

She nods in the darkness and reaches forward to turn on the radio. We listen to Civil Twilight as I push down on the accelerator. Bree is the only one I told about what happened with Ryan. She is the only one who knows why I've changed so much, so quickly. And she knows when I don't want to talk about it. I love her for that.

"Your place, or mine?" I ask.

"Can you take me home? I told my parents Preston would drop me off later. I don't want them to worry." Her voice is tiny as she stares out the window.

"Sure."

I thump my hands on the steering wheel to the beat of the music and ignore the rising number on the speedometer. I have every street in between Bree's house and my apartment memorized. I floor the pedal as we head up a hill and let the car barrel down the other side at nearly fifty miles an hour. A sliver of moon is all that shows in the inky sky and it seems even the stars are hiding.

It's Bree's scream that abruptly yank me out of my music reverie but I see the car backing out of the driveway too late and the front end of my Focus slams into the back of the Honda. The last thing I see as my body is pitched forward into the airbag is Bree's beautiful brown hair billowing out around her before she crashes through the windshield.

CHAPTER 2

It seems like hundreds of people show up for the funeral. But I doubt even half of them actually know who she really was. I feel like I have a scarlet letter sewn in to the front of my shirt. Not everyone knew Bree, but they all know I'm the girl that got her killed. Her mom wouldn't even look at me. Not that I wanted her too.

The breeze has settled around us, which makes the trees at the cemetery look like stocky and still security guards. I stare at them, wondering if they hate me too. Trying not to rub at the small cut above my eyebrow, I squirm in my scratchy black dress, tugging in aggravation at the too-high collar for some relief from the heat. For the first time that I can remember, I resent the warmth of the Southern California sun as it beats down on me from above, burning my nose and scalp where my hair is parted.

Dad ushers me around the somber faced and raven-dressed crowd after the funeral, doing his best to shield me from the angry and sad looks, I guess. It doesn't matter really because nothing anyone says or does will make me feel any worse than I already do. Lovely Bree. My best friend, the only one who truly knew me, and she's gone…all because of me.

♥

"She's cutting herself again!" Dad yells into the phone.

I cringe from behind my closed bedroom door, not wanting to hear the conversation he is having with my mother. Honestly, if she cared, she would have come home the first time he called her about my 'problem'. His voice lowers and now all I can hear is the echo of his garbled tone from the other side of the house. *Whatever.*

I flop down onto my bed and burry my head into the pillows. I want to fall asleep and never wake up. I miss Bree, and I have no one else to talk to about her. I also have no desire to go to college in the fall, though Dad insists on it. The last thing I want is more school. From underneath one of the pillows I rub my hand along my arm, where the newest cut is starting to scab over. I have six scars now. Sometimes I think they are beautiful and other times they just remind me of the pain, and that's when I cut again. I can't help it.

The therapist urges me to write when I feel like cutting myself, 'Journal' as she calls it. What a joke. Dad insisted I go after Bree died and we've spent weeks talking about nothing, and then what happened with Ryan just sort of slipped out. She has me almost convinced that not all boys are the same and encourages me to try dating when I'm ready. Dating. Yeah, right. Even if I wanted to go on a date, there's no one I like, no one I *trust*.

I spring upright when Dad throws my door open and I glare at him. "Can't you knock?"

He tosses the phone onto my mattress before walking away. "She wants to talk to you."

I pick the phone up and hold it limply to my ear. "Yeah?"

"Piper. Is it true, are you…hurting yourself again?" My Mom asks with a deep sigh as if I'm boring her. Typical.

"I'm fine Mom."

"That's not what your dad is saying," she snaps, and then softens her tone a bit. "Honey, I wish you could tell us what's going on. Is this about Bree?"

I stiffen when I hear her name. "No. I'm fine Mom."

There's a pause and then a long sigh on the other side of the phone. "Okay, let me talk to your father."

I get up and carry the receiver into the living room where Dad is sitting, sulking on the couch in front of the TV, where he is most evenings.

"She wants to talk to you." After tossing the phone into his lap, I return to the familiar solitary confinement of my room. I climb under the comforter with my clothes on and pull the sheets up over my head. I just want to go back to sleep.

When I open my eyes, the sun is bright behind my orange curtains and I groan in protest. I roll away from the window and catch a glimpse of myself in the full length mirror that hangs from the inside of my bedroom door. My eyes look a greenish-brown today and my hair hangs around my face limply. It's an unfamiliar and desolate face staring back at me. I pucker my pale lips at my reflection, hoping the pout will bring some color back to my mouth but when that doesn't work I bite down on them until they turn a rosy red color. *Better.*

I hear my cell ping with a text message alert so I roll over onto my stomach to reach for the phone. I haven't used it much since Bree died, but since no one really calls me, my curiosity is piqued. The muscles in my face go slack when I open up the text. It's from an unavailable number. And says only one word: MURDERER.

I throw the phone across the room and fling myself back onto the bed, burrowing under the covers once again. I pray for sleep to take me but instead the tears begin to flow and I cry into my pillow until it's damp. I can't control my moods. Every five minutes I'm angry, sad, bitter, weak, defeated, broken, or vengeful. I feel ugly from the inside out, always.

Eventually, I roll onto my back and stare up at the ceiling fan as the blades make their slow rotations around the room and my mind takes me to dark places; places I don't want to go, but can't seem to keep myself away from lately. *What's the point in fighting it?*

Dad is at work, which means the house is empty for at least another six hours. I get up and wash my face in the bathroom. Suddenly, I'm tempted to brush my teeth, something I haven't bothered to do for three days. I open the cabinet and one of Dad's medicine bottles catches my eye. I reach inside and slowly remove the bottle, shaking it gently in my hand. It's full. *Perfect.*

A few minutes later I sit down at my desk, with a piece of paper in my hand and my favorite blue pen with the chewed cap. I left my window open and the warm summer air flutters through the curtains, gently caressing my skin. For a while I rub the fresh bandage on my arm and blink at the bright day outside. Tears prickle at the edges of my eyes and start cascading down my cheeks, dripping off my chin and plopping onto the paper in fat splats. I hate that I cry all the time now. *I hate it.* I lick my lips and take a deep breath before scribbling two words onto the paper:

I'm Sorry.

Taking a big gulp of air, I push away from the desk quickly and accidentally knock the empty bottle of Diazepam onto the floor. After picking it up, I carefully place it next to the paper before walking over to the window to peer into the too-bright sunshine. In the courtyard below there are two young boys riding their bikes and an older woman sitting alone by the pool, watching them. She's wearing a bright yellow hat and every time she looks up at the children, the glare from her hat forces me to squint. I can smell BBQ from somewhere nearby and inhale it deeply. It mixes oddly with the cucumber-melon smell of a candle I have near the window, but I like it…the smells conflict with each other…sort of like everything else in my life.

Nothing since Ryan Burke has been easy. Everything since Bree's death has been unbearable.

When my eyes feel heavy and my body is sleepy, I crawl into bed and pull the covers up tight around me. After fluffing my pillow until it's comfy, I snuggle into it, being careful to keep my hair tucked neatly around my head. My eyelids feel heavy and I blink slowly, looking around my room, watching the curtains sway in the breeze, feeling hollow and empty inside. I'm dying to forget it all.

Before I close my eyes, I remember Bree's funeral and all the people that came to say goodbye to her. *No one will go to my funeral.* That's the last thought I have before the light is gone and the darkness swallows me.

CHAPTER 3

I groan at the bright light behind my closed eyes, hoping that if I squeeze my lids tight enough the light won't get through. It doesn't work. *What am I lying on?* I'm flat on my back, on something hard and...cold. *Where am I? Oh no. It didn't work. I'm in the hospital! Crap.* With that thought my eyes fly wide open and I bolt upright. Disoriented from the blinding glow around me, I almost fall off a bench.

I steady myself, gripping the edge of the cool marble surface as I swing my naked legs slowly around until my feet touch the ground. I jerk them upwards immediately, surprised by how cold the ground is. Everywhere I look it's the same white light. I can't tell if I'm inside or outside and my stomach clenches with anxiety.

"Hello?" I whisper at first.

The sound of my small voice echoes softly around me, but no one responds. I'm hesitant to place my bare feet on the ground again which oddly feels like glass, but I do, and though it's still cold the initial shock wears off quickly. Slowly and cautiously, I stand up and my hair cascades around my shoulders, loose, clean and smelling like...*grapefruit*? I reach up to touch it and run my hand along the smooth strands. When I went to bed my hair was not this clean. *What's going on?*

"Hello, is anyone there?"

After hearing no response, I step away from the hard bench and turn in a semi-circle...nothing to see but the dazzling whiteness. I can't tell where the top meets the bottom of the room...if it *is* a room I'm standing in. I reach up to rub my arm unconsciously and gasp as I realize not only are my bandages gone but my cuts are healed. I hold my forearm up to my face and rub my hand along my skin. It's soft and smooth...scar-free. *What the hell?* This is when I start to panic. Tears build up in my eyes and I open my mouth to scream but a gentle male voice behind me startles me into silence.

"Piper Willow?"

I whirl around to see a middle-aged man with grey hair smiling politely at me. The first thing I notice is his outdated clothing. He's wearing a blue argyle sweater vest with a long-sleeved white shirt rolled up to his elbows, and pleated brown trousers with matching loafers. I gape at him, sure that I don't know him while he nods sympathetically at me. He's holding a metal clipboard and he taps one of his fingers down on it before speaking again.

"You are Piper Willow, yes?" He raises one of his bushy eyebrows at me.

"Um...yeah."

I tug at the bottom hem of my long tank top, wishing I was wearing more than my pajamas. I feel exposed and naked standing before this stranger. He seems to relax a bit after I answer and he thrusts a hand out in front of him for me to shake. I take it weakly, letting him pump my arm twice.

"Piper, my name is Niles...Niles Abbott. And I need you to come with me please."

He smiles his gentle smile again and even though I don't know him, I feel...*safe*. My feet make soft sounds on the cold, glassy surface of the ground as I follow the strange man through the blinding light. How he can see where he's going, I have no idea. I stay close behind him, afraid that if he gets too far ahead of me, I will lose sight of him.

"Excuse me, Niles...I mean, Mr. Abbott. But, where are we?"

"I'll explain everything to you dear, just as soon as we reach the Station." His answer attempts to be reassuring. His patient voice is calm and matter-of-fact but I'm not comforted, not in the least.

"What station? We aren't in the hospital? Where's my Dad?"

My last question comes out barely above a whisper as I struggle not to cry. Niles startles me as he turns around and smiles, obviously aware of information I don't have yet.

"No Piper, this isn't the hospital, and your father is at home...he's fine. Please, follow me."

He turns away and continues on through the light. I hang my head, staring at my bare feet as we walk. Even though my cuts are gone, I keep rubbing my arm. It's soothing. I almost bump into Niles when he stops abruptly.

"We're here," he says softly.

I look up to see a long and rusty metal gate, entwined with flowering vines and two giant redwood trees standing at each end, like towering guards. I stare at the massive trunks in awe. I've never seen a tree so tall before. The redwoods reach up so high that the tops dissolve into the surrounding incandescence. Niles steps aside and gestures for me to approach the gate.

"Ladies first." He smiles.

I think I blush in embarrassment as I pass him and step up to the large gate with trepidation. I have no idea how to open it but I place my hands on it and it glides easily to the side. I push harder until there is enough room for both me and Niles to pass through, grinning wildly at him as if I've discovered the cure to cancer while he nods at me in approval. After he steps in behind me, I tug on the gate to close it. It easily slides into place with a satisfying clank.

The blinding white light is muted but not gone. As I turn around I find myself in a courtyard of sorts. I can't see the sky, but I guess that we are outside. There are several sterile looking buildings lined up in a curved row, facing us. I gape at them as I read the simple block letters printed above the doors.

The Admissions Department is the largest building and it sits just in front of us. To the right is the Training Department and next to that is a much smaller building labeled "Staff Only". On the other side of the Admissions building is an equally impressive structure - Consignment Department, according to the sign. A smaller building sits on the far end and I think I see children running around inside it. *What is this place?* I so badly want answers. I can't see beyond the buildings...there just seems to be a wall of white behind them, though not as blinding as where I woke up.

"Where am I?" I ask Niles, still sweeping my eyes across the buildings and the people moving in and out of them. And there are a lot of people. Hundreds, I think...maybe even more.

"Piper, this is the Station. I'm your Intake Specialist."

"Intake Specialist?" I whisper, not understanding. At all.

He gestures for me to walk beside him and I match his slow pace as we stroll around an immense water fountain that takes up a good amount of space between the gate and the Admissions Department building. Despite its significant size, the design is simple. It's the blue tile that I find so attractive. I gaze at the rim, wide enough to use as a seat, and the inside of the fountain...following the turquoise tile that rolls up and down in a wave pattern. It's breathtaking and for a moment I forget completely that Niles is talking to me.

"Piper? Are you listening? It's important that you hear me now." His voice is gentle, not at all authoritative. I nod at him, embarrassed.

"Let's sit down, shall we?" He points at a marble bench very much like the one I awoke on.

"Is this place real?" I ask Niles as I sit down. The marble feels cool against the back of my thighs.

"Of course it is." He laughs softly, before his expression turns serious. "Piper, what is the last thing you remember?"

"Remember?" I scrunch my face together as I struggle to remember something...anything. My memories feel fuzzy and faraway at first, but slowly, as if a fog lifts from my mind, I begin to see my bedroom. The pale purple walls that hadn't been painted since I was fourteen come into focus....and my bedspread...I see the yellow quilt with its pink border and myself lying motionless in my bed.

"I remember my bedroom," I say quietly, as a feeling of dread spreads through my body.

Niles' full head of grey hair moves slowly with an empathic nod. "Yes, your bedroom," he pauses to look up at me before taking my hand into his. "It's where you died, dear."

I feel my lower jaw drop open and I stare at Niles like a unicorn horn sprouted from his forehead. But just before I begin to argue, I see my bedroom again and me sitting at my desk writing the last two words I thought of to tell my Dad. And the pills. *Oh my god, the pills.* I blink slowly and realize that Niles is rubbing my hand.

"I'm...*dead*?"

"Yes dear. You are dead." He emphasizes each word carefully, clearly hoping I hear each one.

"No way."

Niles cocks his head to one side and looks at me curiously. He seems surprised, but I don't think he understands I'm in shock. I must be. I can't really be dead, can I?

"So, if I'm dead, where am I? Is this Heaven?" I look away from my hands to peek up at him.

He nods his head slowly. "No."

I feel the color drain from my face. "Is this Hell?"

Niles smiles patiently at me, again with that knowing expression.

"No, this isn't Hell, dear. Think of this place as a sort of spiritual weigh-station for those who volunteer to move on."

"What do you mean...*move on*?"

"For those who have committed suicide, dear."

I inhale sharply as Niles pats my hand reassuringly. "Not all cases, of course. Otherwise this place would be completely over-run."

He waves a hand in front of him casually while he talks but looks around us with a loving expression. I think three things at that moment...*Crap. I really did it, I killed myself. How long has Niles been here? When will I finally pass out?* I pull my hand from his and grip my legs, lowering my head between my knees. I feel the sudden urge to pass out.

Just breathe, Piper. Breathe.

"Piper, I know this is a lot to take in. I think I should take you to the Admissions Department now, they will take care of you there." He pats my back and then stands.

I'm sure I won't be able to walk but when I sit upright my head isn't fuzzy and my knees don't knock together like I expect when I take the first few steps away from the bench. I remember I'm barefoot and look down at my pajama shorts with shame.

"Don't worry about your clothes, Piper." He stops to chuckle. "Some people arrive in just their birthday suit."

CHAPTER 4

I stand inside the Admissions Department, amazed at how long the hallway is. The floor feels just as cold inside as it did outside, but now it has more of a milky color to it. I want to reach down and touch it; almost sure my hand will come up wet, but since Niles is standing next to me, urging me to move down the wide hallway, I'm afraid to stop.

There are large blue doors every few feet and I try not to bump into people as they mingle around us. A tall man, so thin that I can see the outline of his ribcage beneath his frayed grey t-shirt almost passes by us in a flurry, a metal clipboard in hand. He raises a dark eyebrow at me and pauses only slightly to greet Niles.

"New arrival, Abbott?" He asks.

"Yes, this is Piper Willow." He turns toward me and gestures at the rushed man standing awkwardly in the hall. "Piper, this is Mr. Carlson Smith."

I smile shyly at Carlson, who is still staring at me with his eyebrow raised in a high arc. I know he's not impressed. He nods curtly at me, before glancing down at his clipboard, hugging it tightly to his chest.

"I'm late for the gate. Another newbie."

"Till later then." Niles nods a friendly dismissal and Carlson scurries off.

I follow Niles almost to the end of the hallway, until he opens one of the large blue doors, waving me inside. A wide blue counter runs the length of the room and there are three privacy walls set up, as well as three individual lines to stand in. Besides Niles and the portly woman with the tight bun sitting behind the counter at the middle partition, there is only one other girl in the room. When we enter, she turns and smiles nervously at me, then resumes her quiet discussion with Tight Bun Lady.

"Have a seat, Piper. Mrs. Ferdinand will be with you shortly." Niles says to me with a smile.

"Wait, are you leaving?" I start to panic at the thought of being alone with Tight Bun Lady...er, Mrs. Ferdinand.

Crap.

"I will see you later, Piper. But now I have other work to do."

Double crap.

He winks at me before closing the heavy blue door behind him. I look around the room, trying to control my nerves and rub at my left forearm until I'm sure the skin is raw. When I glance down, my arm isn't raw...it's not even red. *Hmm.* I tug my loose fitting tank top over my hips, trying to hide the shortness of my cotton pajama bottoms.

I hear the chair squeak softly on the hard floor in front of me and the young Asian girl with the nervous smile stands and says something to Tight Bun Lady that I can't make out. When she turns away from the counter, she is hugging a white piece of paper to her chest. She smiles shyly at me as she walks by and I wonder how old she is…at least two years younger than me. Her yellow sundress flows around her knees as she squeezes through the blue door…and then she's gone. I'm still staring after her when Tight Bun Lady curtly says my name.

"Piper Willow?" She smiles but it doesn't show in her eyes.

I approach her cautiously and clear my throat before speaking. "Um, yes."

"Have a seat."

She nods at the chair in front of me. I sit down in it a little too hard and she scowls slightly. My cheeks flush and I pin my hands in between my knees to keep them from shaking as I process how terrifying Tight Bun Lady must have been before she came to the Station. She was probably a Librarian. The thought makes me giggle and I clamp my teeth down onto my lower lip to keep the sound in.

"Not many New Arrivals laugh at my desk, Miss Willow."

Oops.

She is staring hard at me, both eyebrows raised first in surprise and then furrowed together with absolute displeasure. Immediately the urge to laugh is gone and I squeeze my knees harder against my hands.

"I'm sorry," I mumble.

My apology seems to please her and she nods while she shuffles papers around on the counter between us. *Paperwork, even after death...how ironic.* The thought makes me want to laugh again and I clamp down hard on my lip once more, hoping Tight Bun Lady didn't catch my near slip again.

"Did Mr. Abbott explain why you are here, Miss Willow?" She looks up from her paperwork to stare blankly at me. I nod, afraid to speak.

"Good. I'm sure you have many questions, but first," she waves one of her hands in front of her face, "...paperwork."

I really can't help it and the laugh is out of my mouth before I can stop it. I quickly bring my hands up to cover it but the look of shock on Tight Bun Lady's face makes the sound in my throat vibrate harder between my lips, spilling out around my fingers. She slowly leans back into her chair and purses her lips together tightly and my mind screams, *Librarian!* I only laugh harder; now I have to lean forward, and grip my stomach while I struggle to catch my breath. When I'm done I'm winded as if I ran up a flight of stairs. Tight Bun Lady looks very, very unhappy with me.

I wipe a tear from my eye and take in several ragged breaths before she speaks.

"Are you quite done now, Miss Willow?"

"I'm sorry. It's just...*paperwork*...here? You don't find that funny?" I smile at her.

She leans forward onto the counter and steeples her chubby fingers in front of her. Her large bosom rests against the edge of the wide desk and her tight bun pulls at the corners of her eyes, stretching her skin tight. My smile fades as she stares icily at me.

"No, Miss Willow, I do not find paperwork funny. If you're finished with your outburst, I'd like to continue my job now. Would that be okay with you, or do you need another moment to compose yourself accordingly?"

Oh, it's like this is it?

Tight Bun Lady has absolutely no more patience with me. I squirm in my chair while she shuffles the papers between us once more and pulls something from the pile, setting it in front of me. It looks like a checklist:

WELCOME TO THE STATION

Please follow the checklist in this guide to help accommodate you with the purpose of the Station. We value each and every person that passes through our gates, whether you choose to move on or become a Volunteer. If you ever need assistance please request a meeting with your Intake Specialist. Remember, everyone deserves a second chance. Please do the following:

- Complete your appropriate paperwork with the Admissions Department
- Attend your Life In Review meeting (First Door of Admissions Department)
- Attend Orientation

- Locate your Intake Specialist for further instructions

What?! What the hell is a Volunteer*? Move on? To where?!* I look up at Tight Bun Lady and she smiles broadly at my confused expression.

"So...Miss Willow, let's get you processed, shall we?"

♀

I can't help fidgeting with the edge of my checklist as I sit in the lobby of the Review room. The large, open space reminds me of a church, though instead of pews, sturdy chairs sit neatly next to each other. Half of the chairs are full and at the front of the room, instead of where a church podium would be, there are three doors. A man, dressed in all black, announces a name every fifteen minutes or so after a person exits one of the three doors...and someone else gets up from their white chair to follow him inside the room. I notice very quickly that no one has returned to the lobby with a dry face.

What exactly happens to them in there?

I've been focusing on the pale beams of the ceiling when the middle door opens and the young girl ahead of me at Admissions comes out. She is weeping softly and passes by me without looking up. The sadness that envelopes her is a stark contrast to her happy sundress that dances wildly around her legs as she rushes out of the room.

"Piper Willow." The man in black announces stoically.

I gulp and rise on shaky legs, bumping into the person sitting in front of me as I step out into the center aisle. The walk is long and I feel as if every set of eyes behind me is boring into my back. I tell myself I won't come out crying.

I won't.

"This way, please." He ushers me into the middle room and now I can see it's empty. Confused, I turn to look at him as he pulls the door shut behind me with only a slight nod.

Wait! What happens in this room?!

I stand completely still. The small square room is all walls with no windows. Only a single white light bulb hangs from the center of the ceiling. I'm waiting for the walls to close in around me, or the floor to drop, when I hear her voice.

Mom.

For what seems like hours, the walls flash vividly around me with every monumental moment in my life...from my birth, to my first birthday; the hospital visit after falling off my bike when I was eight, followed by a trip to the ice cream shop to celebrate my first cast; Dad hugging me to his chest every night for a month after Mom left; my Tumbling performances; Bree smiling; Ryan Burke dumping something into my beer at the party; Bree flying through the windshield because I didn't tell her to put a seatbelt on...and the last day of my life. I see it play out in slow motion, me tossing back handfuls of Dad's sleeping pills, me staring out the window, me taking my last shallow breath. The last thing I see is a close-up of Dad as he kneels at my bedside, crying into my hair as I lie motionless in my bed.

The walls are suddenly just walls again and my body is shaking violently. My face is wet with tears that I wasn't even aware I was shedding, the front of my shirt damp from them. The door opens and the man in black takes my limp hand tugging me from the room. *This is why everyone is crying when they leave here.* I don't look at anyone as I stumble down the aisle, wanting nothing more but to get the hell out of this place.

Outside, the monotonous white around me suddenly makes me angry and I step back into the slightly darker Admissions Department hallway. I slide down the wall, crumpling onto the floor in a heap of skinny limbs and ash-blonde hair. I stay like this until I hear the soothing and gentle sound of Niles Abbott's voice above me.

CHAPTER 5

"Piper, come walk with me. You'll feel better soon."

I try to nudge his hand off my shoulder, but Niles lifts my arm and pulls me to my feet. My face is still buried in my hands and I don't want to look at him.

"Everyone here has been through this, trust me, you'll be okay." He says gently.

I finally glance up at him. "Really...everyone here has..." My voice trails off as he nods.

"Yes, dear. That is what we all have in common here."

"Oh."

He nudges me again and I follow him back outside...though I'm still not sure what to call it because there's no sky and no ground besides the cold milky glass that I am still walking barefoot on.

"Where can I get a pair of shoes?" I ask him, embarrassed.

"Shoes?" He stops to look down at me. "Are your feet uncomfortable?" He asks carefully.

"Oh…" I blink up at him, and then down at my feet. *Are they uncomfortable?* "No, I guess not."

Niles smiles and starts walking again. I realize he's guiding me toward the smaller building on the end with the children inside, just pass the Consignment Department. I still don't know what all the buildings are for, but I feel relieved when I hear children laughing. He walks straight up to one of several large bay windows and leans forward. I copy him, and peer into the room behind the slightly rainbow-tinted glass.

The smallest child I see looks to be about ten years old and he is chasing an older girl…maybe twelve, around the room while singing a lullaby. They look happy, content; not at all busy and rushed like the adults I've seen around the rest of the Station.

Why are there children here? Niles said everyone here has died…from suicide…did I understand him correctly? Suddenly, I need to know.

"Niles, you said everyone here shares something in common. What *exactly* did you mean?"

I ask the question without taking my gaze off the small boy running around the large room. I hear him sigh softly before he speaks.

"Piper, everyone here at the Station has committed suicide. We've all chosen to end our lives. And even children as young as Victor there can make that choice."

"That's so…*sad*." My eyes fill with tears again.

42

"Yes, it is. But it's different for them. We call children under thirteen *Ones*. They will move on from this place after only a little while. Honestly, I think they are here just briefly enough to give those of us older folks some genuine happiness. Children can do that, after all."

"What do you mean...you *think*? Don't you know where they go?" I turn to look at him now, astounded and a little scared.

"No Piper. No one here knows what's beyond." He pauses to smile down at me. "But, some of us have our guesses."

Guesses? Are you kidding me?!

He winks and steps away from the window. I don't want to leave the children, Niles was right...they make you feel happy just watching them. But Niles is walking away from the building back towards the center of the Station, where the giant aqua-marine water fountain flows peacefully.

"What do I do now?"

I still have my checklist; it's crumpled and damp from my tears but I haven't lost it yet. I do not want to return to see Tight Bun Lady for another copy, so I hold onto the piece of paper as if my after-life depends on it.

"What's next on your list, Piper?" Niles asks me gently.

"Um...*Attend Orientation*." I look up at him expectantly.

"Orientation it is, then." He smiles and walks me next door into the Consignment Department building. It's much like the Admissions Department, the same long hallway with several doors that line the hall, except these doors are a faded green, instead of blue. He pauses at the very first door, with his slightly wrinkled hand on the knob.

"I can't attend Orientation with you, dear, but you will see me when you are finished, okay?"

"Okay." The word comes out a squeak and I hesitantly walk through the door when he holds it open for me with a smile.

"You'll be fine. Just choose what you feel is right." He quickly pulls the door shut behind him.

Oh no. Choose what's right?

My stomach twists in a ball of restless nerves as I turn slowly around to face the open room. There is another small hallway in front of me, with two closed doors on my left and two closed doors on my right. I feel my knees bang together as I replay the last thing Niles told me. *Just choose what you feel is right.* I reach out to touch the first door to my left when the one immediately across from it opens with a flurry.

"Oh no, honey. That room is currently in session."

A short woman wearing a long, white nightgown smiles at me from under a ginormous coif of rust-colored hair. I'm completely lost in the pile of curls on her head, that at first I don't hear a thing she says.

"Honey?"

She tilts her head to the side and smiles up at me again. *How does her hair not fall off her head?* I ask myself, in disbelief. I smile back and thrust my hand out for her to shake while I introduce myself.

"Piper Willow." We smile at each other for a brief moment and then she quickly ushers me into the tiny room she came from.

"We've been waiting for you, Piper," she says sweetly as she takes my narrow shoulders and guides me to an empty chair at the back of the packed room.

At least twenty faces turn to glance at me and I notice all of them are teenagers. I spot the girl in the yellow sundress and we smile at each other. She is sitting two rows in front of me, next to another girl, perhaps about her age who is wearing a long black shift dress.

Interesting outfit to die in. I think to myself.

"Okay, class. Now that our last New Arrival has...well, arrived," a few of the boys laugh at the unintended joke, "...we can start with your Orientation."

Mrs. Sweet Big Hair looks at me with a nod and even though I temporarily feel put on the spot, I don't feel uncomfortable - in fact, Mrs. Sweet Big Hair makes me feel welcome and relaxed. She reminds me of Niles, though they look nothing alike. I sit back in my chair and take a moment to scan the room. What's interesting is that most of the boys are fully clothed, with one exception...a thin young man, about my age, who is wearing nothing but pajama pants. Suddenly, I don't feel as naked as I did before.

"So, I know most of you are confused, maybe even upset about being here. My job is to explain to you how the Station works and what your options are."

My interest is instantly piqued. I lean forward in my chair, as does most of my fellow 'classmates' while we listen to Mrs. Sweet Big Hair tell us why we are here.

"I won't be able to answer all of your questions, but I can tell you each one of you has a choice to make." She smiles at the room sweetly. I can't imagine anything depressing this woman enough to take her own life, she's too darn happy.

"The Station serves two *very* important purposes. We help many people move on to their next journey of course, but most importantly, we help those in need."

Those in need.

I furrow my brows together, clearly confused. The boy next to me squirms in his seat and he too looks confused and maybe a little worried. For the first time I notice the ceiling matches the milky floor...it's not exactly moving, but it reminds me of something organic.

"See, when you chose to end your life...you took a path that landed you here. Think of it as a fork in the road that wasn't meant to be there. Anyhoo, now you are here and you can either return back," there is a collective gasp in the room, "...or, you can opt-out...and move on to your own version of what some of us call Hell." Every bottom in the room wiggles around nervously in their seat.

A chunky boy with small, beady eyes interrupts her, "What do you mean go back?"

"Well, it's not quite what you think," she says, with that sweet smile again. "You can't return back to *your* life. You died, remember? What you *can* do is volunteer to go back as the temporary subconscious of a person in need."

I tilt my head to the side at the same time as the person in front of me. I feel my heart-rate quicken.

This is not what I expected...at all.

"If you do become a Volunteer, as most New Arrivals do, you will go through training, and be given an assignment...a person within your age range that is dangerously depressed or hurting enough to end their own life. It is the Volunteer's job to keep this person safe from self-injury. This is our way of giving back. You can see, hear, and feel everything through your assignment, but they are never aware of your presence and despite how hard you try, they will not always hear *you*. Volunteers stay with each assignment until they are no longer needed. Either the person dies, or they improve to a point where they can handle life on their own once again. When that happens, Volunteers return here to the Station for a new case. And so goes your existence until you are ready to move on."

No way.

She raises her hand to quell the flurry of interruptions and the group becomes instantly quiet again. I glance around the room, and I'm sure my face mirrors the perplexed and terrified expressions of those around me.

"Now. If you do not wish to become a Volunteer, you have only one other option. You can opt-out." She says the last two words with reverence. "You must understand though that everything that pushed you to end your life follows you...the pain, the sorrow, the loss, the guilt, the hopelessness. With those feelings, you spend the rest of your existence. Alone." She pauses, takes a deep breath, and then says in a quiet voice, "Only the strongest and bravest New Arrivals elect this option."

The room stills around me. Now I understand why she said most people choose to become Volunteers. I ended my life because I couldn't handle the pain and the guilt...spending eternity with it would be just...unbearable.

That's not an option.

We sit, mesmerized by Mrs. Sweet Big Hair, as she goes into full detail about both of our 'options'. Niles stated clearly that this place wasn't Hell, but both of these choices seem like punishment to me. Before Orientation is over, I know which one I will choose and it's an easy choice for me to make because I'm not strong...or brave.

Not anymore.

I stand in the short line behind Yellow Sundress Girl...waiting for Mrs. Sweet Big Hair to pass me my Orientation Pass. I'm to take it next door to the Training Department immediately. After she places the small rectangular object in my hand, I turn it over once, noticing no markings on the smooth red glass surface. She nods kindly at me and shakes my hand before I turn to leave the room.

Standing in the far corner is a boy much taller than me. He wears all black clothing and his dark hair lies limply on top of his head. He glares at the room and makes no effort to get in line for a pass. I move very slowly from the front of the room, back to the door, letting Mrs. Sweet Big Hair reach him first.

"Jeremy," she says to him, with a soft look in her eyes, "have you made a decision?"

"I won't go back." He says the words flatly.

I see her nod, understanding on her face. But I've reached the door now and if I don't go through it, they will both know I'm hovering. I open it slowly and risk a final glance at the tall young man before I hear Mrs. Sweet Big Hair talk again.

"If this is what you want, I can help you move on, Jeremy."

"I can't go back. I won't do it." His voice is strained, tight with emotion.

"Okay. You'll have to come with me."

Wow.

Trish Marie Dawson

CHAPTER 6

"Come on everyone, quiet down. Attention, please!"

The room settles into an uneasy hush. I stand near the back, two people away from Yellow Sundress Girl. The Training Department lobby is massive. And just as I expected it looks like the other main buildings except the entryway is much wider. *To accommodate group arrivals?*

"I need teens through door one, twenties through door two, thirties through door three, forties through door four...you get the picture?"

A hairy man with a portly belly is weaving through the crowd of people...pointing at doors and answering questions in little quips. I bet he's wished a million times he chose a different last outfit. His too-tight tee shows the fold of his under belly and his boxer shorts sag crookedly on his wide hips.

Poor guy. Guess that could explain his pissy demeanor.

"So, this is our room?"

There's a timid high-pitched voice to my right and I turn to find Yellow Sundress Girl standing at my elbow. In front of us is a closed, red door simply marked: *ONE.* I know that the first thing we will do behind this door is attend a crash Therapy course. A chance to pick a part the choice me made that ended us all here. I am not looking forward to Therapy in the after-life, *at all.*

I smile broadly at the younger girl standing beside me and she relaxes her shoulders a bit. I think I've made her nervous for some reason. Her almond shaped eyes are dark brown but inviting, and her short, black hair is silkier than anything I've seen before. The rich honey-color of her Asian skin goes perfectly with the happy hue of her dress. As I look at her I think she's quite beautiful and I wonder what it was in her life that made her want to leave it.

"I'm Piper." I smile at her.

"My name is Kerry-Anne." She returns a shy smile.

"Nice to meet you, Kerry-Anne."

The chunky boy with beady eyes brushes rudely past me and leans forward to open the large, red door. In his hurry, he steps on one of my bare feet, which surprisingly doesn't hurt but he continues on as if nothing happened. I glare at his back rolls and stick my tongue out while Kerry-Anne giggles softly, covering her mouth with one of her dainty hands.

As Beady Eyes goes into the room first, I silently ask why he's so anxious for the next step. All I really want to do is find somewhere dark and quiet to hide in for a while. Kerry-Anne tugs softly on my hand, pulling me into the room behind her which snaps me out of my self-wallowing. I think instantly that we will become good friends.

♥

I feel like I've been emotionally and physically drained, stripped and prodded for centuries by the time we are allowed out of our first training session. Kerry-Anne seems just as overwhelmed when we make our way out of the building and find ourselves drawn to the fountain. We sit on the edge, a few feet away from three other girls we trained with.

"I don't think I can do this," Kerry-Anne says softly.

"Sure you can. I mean, we have to." I try and smile at her.

"But what if I totally fail...*again*?" She's looking down at her hands.

Fail...again?

"Remember what our trainer said...we won't get our first case until they know we are ready." I pat her hands and she twitches before looking up at me with sad, brown eyes.

I sigh. I don't want to admit out-loud that I have my own self-doubts. I glance around at the groups of people that hover around the buildings, and the few that seem on a mission...walking briskly from one place to another. That's when I spot Niles coming toward the fountain and I grin at him. I'm beyond happy to see a friendly face.

"Niles!" I stand to hug him as he approaches and he pats me lightly on the back.

"So, I see you have decided to stay and become a Volunteer?"

I nod, but my face must give away my doubts because he leans forward and playfully pinches one of my cheeks.

"You will make a great Volunteer." His gentle smile warms me.

I turn sideways so that Niles is facing Kerry-Anne.

"Kerry-Anne, this is Niles Abbott...my Intake Specialist."

She stands shyly and nods at Niles, who grins but doesn't offer his hand. He must know she takes some warming up to, but his smile seems to ease her nerves some.

"It's very nice to meet you, Kerry-Anne."

"You too." Her quiet, mumbled reply is barely audible.

"Kerry-Anne, mind if I borrow Piper for just a minute?"

"No, of course not." Her eyes widen, as if I'm in trouble.

"Everything's fine. I'll return her to you momentarily." He smiles his perfect Niles Smile and I follow him pass the Training Department to the much smaller staff building.

When he pushes open the front door, I stand awkwardly behind him unsure of what it is he wants me to do.

"It's okay Piper, there's someone who wants to meet you and this is the most private place available right now." He urges me inside and closes the door behind us. I jump as the large piece of wood clunks into place.

"Have I done something wrong?" I ask timidly.

"Oh, gosh no! I'm sorry; I didn't mean to worry you. Here, come this way."

My naked feet pad softly on the cold floor as I follow him around a corner and through a small open doorway. There is a large conference style table sitting in the center of the room and a startlingly beautiful girl about my age sitting with her elbows resting on the table. When we enter the room she stands abruptly and looks nervously between me and Niles. She's wearing a long-sleeve sweater the color of pink bubblegum that hugs her curves and a short pleated skirt. I think *'Cheerleader'* and instantly dislike her.

Confused, I look up at Niles who is smiling down at me. "Piper, this is Mallory Storm. She was your Volunteer."

My Volunteer?

Mallory's breath hitches as my face falls. She hasn't moved from her spot at the table and I'm not sure I want her to come near me. Am I mad at her for failing me...or should I be grateful she tried at all?

I am so confused.

"I don't understand." I say just above a whisper...aiming the question at Niles.

"Piper, usually Volunteers don't meet their assignments, but when you arrived Mallory insisted on it. I'll wait outside in the hall for you, okay?" Niles says calmly.

"You're leaving me here…with *her*?" I gasp.

For the first time, Niles looks sternly at me, before he says quietly, "Piper, this is a conversation that I believe should be held in private…between only you and Miss Mallory." And with that he leaves the room, closing the door softly behind him.

♀

"Please, sit down," Mallory says, using her hand to gesture at one of the vacant chairs. I notice that her hand is shaking slightly and this makes me just a little bit happy.

"Should I be upset with you?" I'm not sure why I ask the question and it seems to surprise Mallory.

"Well, I guess that feeling could be mutual." She smiles at me, a knowing look in her eyes.

"You think I let *you* down?" I ask incredulously.

Mallory sighs and shifts in her chair. I'm trying not to stare at her features, but her large blue eyes, full and perfectly rosy lips and long blonde hair is a bit distracting. She's the Station's version of a living Barbie doll.

"I do feel as if I let you down. I hope you know that," she says it quietly.

"When did you become my Volunteer?" I ask.

"Just shortly after…Ryan." She brings her gaze up from the table and looks directly at me.

I inhale sharply. "Ryan? You know about that?"

"Of course, Piper. I was in your head for several months. I know pretty much everything."

My mouth falls open and I'm sure my jaw has hit the floor. When I register the fact that my tongue is still attached and working, I swallow...hard.

"I don't like the idea of someone being in my head," I say a bit harshly and Mallory flinches.

"But Piper - that is what you've just volunteered to do."

Oh. Crap. She's right. I hate that she's right.

I glare down at my hands, which I've been twisting in my lap. It was a habit my Dad hated. I take a deep breath and set my hands calmly on the table top. I let the coolness of the blue-tinted glass run through my skin and imagine it cooling the rising heat of my face.

"Then you know...*everything*?" I look up at her cautiously.

"Yes. Everything. I know you better than Niles does. And Niles knows a lot." She smiles and I'm sure she's a bit embarrassed.

"This is so weird." I mumble to myself.

"I wanted you to know that I tried very hard for you Piper. I really wish things had...ended...differently for you." I glare at her but I notice when I do that her eyes are beginning to water.

No way. She's going to cry? For me?

At once I feel like a jerk for making her feel bad. I know after my first training session that Volunteers have no actual control over their assignments. This wasn't Mallory's fault, it was mine. Only mine.

"I don't...*remember* you," I admit quietly.

"Well, you wouldn't. From your perspective I was just the nagging voice inside your head. But you are a very stubborn woman, Piper. It was hard for you to hear me." She laughs then, which makes me smile. Because she's right...I'm very stubborn. Always have been, probably always will be.

Her face darkens a bit and somehow I know what she's going to say. "I'm so sorry about Bree. I really liked her."

Now it's my turn to cry. I blink rapidly, hoping that keeps the tears from spilling out onto my cheeks, but one manages to escape. Its salty trail trickles over my lips before I have a chance to wipe it away. I can't speak, so I just nod my head. Mallory gets up slowly from her chair and walks around the table, sitting down carefully into the seat next to me.

"Listen, Piper. You've been through a lot. More than any eighteen year old should have to. I know more than anyone what it feels like to be in your situation. Remember, we were match for a reason? We can't go back and change the past, but we can make a difference with the future for others."

Her words are like a soft blanket draped around my shoulders and I look up at her with a small smile. She's right of course...again. I can't go back and change the past, even though I know I would do it differently if I could. To think how selfish my decision was brings me nearly to tears again. I can't go back and fix my life. But I can make someone else's life better. I could even save someone from themself.

"How long have you been here?" I ask her.

She laughs that throaty perfect laugh again. "Oh Piper, I have no idea. But I've handled 72 cases. I admit I took a bit of a break after your case." She says the last sentence quietly and looks down at her hands.

I can't stop myself from blurting out what I know is true. "It wasn't your fault."

She smiles a face-splitting grin before leaning over to hug me. I notice her hair smells like grapefruit, just like mine. I hug her back and when we release we both have tears in our eyes.

"You are going to be such a great Volunteer, Piper. You're a very brave girl."

Me...brave? I hope she's right. Someone else's life will eventually depend on it.

Trish Marie Dawson

CHAPTER 7

It seems like Therapy lasts forever in Training. I've picked apart my experience with Ryan Burke and Bree's death with our Trainer. And surprisingly, my story isn't that much different from the others in my classes. It makes me feel like less of a failure and more like a survivor, as ironic as that seems. I know what happened with Ryan wasn't my fault now and that not all young men are like him. Does that change things? Well, not yet, I guess. I can still feel a wall around me when it comes to my thoughts about the opposite sex.

And as for Bree, what happened with her was an accident...careless on my part, but an accident nonetheless. It takes many hugs and sobbing sessions for me to begin to understand this. In time I start to feel stronger but I now have a permanent ache in my heart at the thought of what and who I left behind. I'll never improve if I continue to think about Dad and home, and what I so eagerly left behind in a moment of weakness, so eventually I have to put it away…tucked deeply and safely into my subconscious.

After seven training sessions Niles thinks I'm ready. We are sitting outside near the fountain where we've met after each of my sessions. After I drag my hand through the cool water, creating little waves that reach all the way around the bowl, I finally look up at Niles, who is waiting patiently for me to speak first.

"How did you know you were ready for your first case, Niles?"

"Well, I didn't. I really disliked my trainer. I felt I had to do something else, or I'd go crazy." Niles smiles at me as I gawk at his honest answer.

"Niles Abbott, I didn't think you had an impatient bone in your body!" We both laugh.

"I'm serious though, Piper. I do think you are ready. You've been through most scenarios and you have a good mind. You can figure out what to do if you get stuck. Plus, the most basic rule you already know. From Mallory." He says her name softly.

"Yes. That we can only do our best to guide…and regardless of the outcome it's not our fault if our Assignments fail." I sigh heavily.

I was a failure. Poor Mallory.

"Exactly, my dear." He smiles gently at me. "You know, I haven't seen your friend Kerry-Anne lately. Is she out on her first assignment already?"

"Yes." I beam at Niles. "Just after her third training session."

He nods with a smile. "Perhaps she will return before you go out for the first time."

"That would be nice." I stare at my naked feet. "I guess I can go to the Consignment Department and let them know I'm ready."

"You might still have to wait a bit for the right match, of course." Niles reminds me and I nod in understanding.

"Okay. I'll do it. Feel like walking me there?"

More paperwork. I wonder where they get the paper *from*, considering the only trees I've seen are from the giant redwoods by the front gate. I've learned to not ask myself questions like these too often, or I'd go absolutely insane. The Station is full of a lot of unanswered questions and none of the staff seem too preoccupied with the *why's, how's,* or *what if's*. And they aren't talking freely about them, either.

Inside the second door of the Consignment Department is a large room with a giant counter-top that runs the length of the wide and open space. There are several partitions, at least a dozen I think, and unlike the Admissions Department there are no lines but individual seating areas in front of each partition.

Crap, it's the After-life DMV.

"To sign up, you'll want to wait in the first line, here," Niles tells me. There aren't more than four people sitting in each section. Hopefully this means the wait won't be long.

"Okay. Do you have to go?" I ask him, hoping he will stay with me.

"Yes dear, duty calls."

He gives me a wink and turns to leave the building. I stare at the blue diamond pattern of his sweater vest as he walks away. I wonder how long Niles has been here and make a mental note to ask him when I'm done in line.

I wait only minutes before my name is called. Fortunately, the man behind the counter is much friendlier than Tight Bun Lady was and better looking too. Though his skin is pale, he has bright green eyes and a soft smile. I'm so grateful he's fully clothed, otherwise I'm pretty sure I'd be staring at the muscles he seems to have beneath his t-shirt. I've been allowing myself small moments to appreciate the male form. With a desk between us, I feel safe enough to stare.

"Name, please?" He actually manages to sound as if he hasn't asked this question a thousand times already.

"Piper Willow." I say calmly.

"Hello Piper, my name is Drew. Give me just one second here to find your file, okay?" He nods at me pleasantly as he shuffles through some papers behind the counter where I can't see. His wavy blonde hair shifts around his head and tickles his ears as he moves. He shows a full mouth of perfectly aligned, white teeth when he smiles. I try to blink. I really do.

Stop staring, Piper!

"Ahh. There you are. A relatively New Arrival, is that right, Piper?"

Where did he pull this paperwork from?

I answer, "Yes. I've been waiting for the right time to come in, I guess."

He waves dismissively. "No need to explain, Piper. Volunteering is a very serious job. Not to be taken lightly. We want you to be absolutely ready."

With that comment my fragile confidence goes catapulting at Mach-speed to the floor, shattering into a million pieces. I stare down at my hands, defeated.

Drew senses my change in mood and adds quickly, "Piper, your Training Officer gives you very high marks. And Mr. Abbott speaks very fondly of you." There's that dazzling smile again.

"Really?" *High marks?*

"Yes and if you feel you are in fact ready, I can process your activation paperwork now." He smiles and his teeth sparkle against the white of the room.

I wiggle in my seat and stare at Drew, who is patiently waiting for my decision. "Okay," I squeak.

"Are you sure?" He raises a light brown cyebrow at me.

"Yes." I say with a firmer tone.

I'm ready. I can do this.

"Good," he stands and grabs at the pile of paperwork between us. "I'll be right back."

I watch him walk all the way to the end of the counter, which is enjoyable, to say the least, where an older woman with long brown hair is stamping something. She pauses to look up at him before taking the stack of papers. She riffles through them and then stamps several before handing them back to Drew. I try to act as if I wasn't staring when he returns to our end of the counter.

"All approved. You're all set to go, Piper." He smiles at me while dropping my paperwork into something behind the counter.

Drawers, maybe?

"That's it?" I try not to look too shocked.

"Yep, that's it. Now check in with the billboard on the back wall to see that your profile is active. That will show when your case is ready, your current status, etc. Don't worry; it might be a little while before you are given your first case. We take great pains to ensure each Volunteer is matched properly. Take this with you - it will light up in case you aren't in the building when your new assignment comes in."

I nod at him before standing from the chair to accept the small glass disk that hangs from its long metal chain from his proffered hand. It's clear and I study it to see where it will light up from, but I see nothing inside it.

"Oh, and Piper?"

I look up at Drew once more. "Yes?"

"Good luck." He smiles reassuringly and I start to pick my shattered confidence up off the floor.

"Thanks."

The glass feels cool and refreshing as I against the bay window, watching with absentminded curiosity as the children run around their large playroom. This is where I go when Niles is busy and I'm not in a training session. I looked at my profile in the Consignment Department before heading back outside. It was strange to see my picture on the massive board with my name below it and the status: ACTIVE, WAITING ASSIGNMENT. I was able to find Kerry-Anne's profile too and it read: ACTIVE, ON ASSIGNMENT. I looked for Mallory's profile but couldn't find it on the wall. There has to be thousands of Volunteer's on the board.

Not wanting to sit inside the building and just wait, I came here to watch the kids, figuring I have plenty of time before I'm assigned my first case. They have to match me with the right person, after-all.

I notice that a few of the children from before are missing and there is one that I have not seen yet. He's thin with very dark skin, dressed in car pajamas and less eager to play like the others are, though they keep trying to engage him in some sort of activity like tag or hide and seek. Eventually he pairs up with another boy, about eleven, and they begin a friendly game of dodge ball against two girls around their age. He can't be over ten years old. Somewhere I hope his parents miss him.

I laugh watching them and hope that none of them stay at the Station for long. I'm engrossed in their game when a bright reddish-orange light beams me in the eyes, startling me, and I blink in alarm. I back away and see my reflection. My chest is ablaze.

Am I on fire!?

I pat awkwardly at the front of my shirt and when my fingers brush up against the necklace I grip it, holding it out in front of me as far as the think chain will allow. It's pulsating with light. I instantly relax when I realize I'm not on really on fire. But then my stomach clenches and my heart stops...I have an Assignment.

Already? Niles! Where are you?

♀

My eyes take a moment to adjust to the Consignment hallway after being outside and I have to step around a group of chatting middle-aged women to pass through the doorway where the massive Assignment billboard is displayed. I find my profile immediately, but it says I'm still awaiting my Assignment. I don't remember if Drew told me what to do when my necklace lit up, and I scan the room for a familiar face.

"Piper?"

"Mallory!" I say a silent *Thank You* in my head as she leans forward to give me an awkward hug. "I was starting to freak out. I'm not sure what to do," I tell her.

"Your first?" She looks down at my glowing necklace with reverence.

"Yes. But I don't know where to go." My eyes dart around the room quickly; worried I may get into trouble if I take much longer.

"It's okay, Piper. I'll show you. I just picked up my next case too."

She smiles at me and walks us toward the first available partition. I feel as if I'm cutting in line, but I follow Mallory anyway. The girl behind the counter is startlingly young, maybe even younger than me. She has her straw-colored hair pulled back in a loose pony-tail and is wearing a bright green shirt with a cartoon character on it that I don't recognize. She smiles at Mallory kindly.

"Hi, Mal. Back so soon?"

"Hi again Krista, this is Piper Willow. She just got her first Assignment and needs her card." *Card...what card?*

"First Assignment?" Krista nods at me with the same look of reverence Mallory gave me when she saw my glowing necklace.

"Um, yes." I suddenly feel shy.

"That's awesome." She smiles broadly and asks for my necklace. As soon as it touches her hand, the reddish-orange light disappears and it looks like ordinary glass again.

Very cool.

I see Krista fumbling with something behind the desk and then she produces a smooth, rectangular shaped piece of glass, about the size of my palm, much like the pass I was given for the Training Department. Except this one is black. Now I remember from training what card she was referring to.

"Piper, this is your Assignment Card...please be careful with it, we have only one per case and they are not replaccable." Krista smiles at me while she carefully hands the fragile card over.

I turn it over in my hand and it has the same organic look as the incandescent floor. As if the color wants to swirl and move inside the glass. Now I'm absolutely terrified that I will trip and drop it, so I clutch it to my chest with both hands.

"I can show her to the Depot room, Krista. Thanks."

Mallory smiles fondly at her before guiding me away from the counter. As I turn and smile at Krista, she gives me a toothy grin and a thumbs-up sign.

"Your Intake Specialist usually takes you the first time…do you know where Niles is?" Mallory asks me.

"No."

I wish I did. Right now I could use his gentle demeanor and encouraging words. As we make our way through the room which suddenly seems crowded, I listen to Mallory explain the Depot room and its functions. From what I understand from training, it's an arrival and departure portal. I have no idea how it works and feel too nervous to ask.

We turn left when we exit the room and I follow Mallory as she guides me to the end of the long hallway. As we stop in front of the last door my nerves jerk in my legs.

Mallory takes a deep breath. "This is it…the Depot." She reaches out to hold my hand and squeezes it gently.

"Are you nervous?" My voice is just above a whisper.

"Always a little. Are you?"

"Extremely." We both laugh.

Mallory opens the door and I step carefully over the threshold. I am not sure what to expect, but Mallory seems confidant and relaxed while she tugs me next to her as we approach a long wall, flanked by the only two doors in the small room. There are hundreds of slashes on the white wall, but as we get closer, I see that some are occupied by the same shiny black glass that Mallory and I both hold. They stick out slightly from their docking places in no particular pattern and it reminds me of a rock climbing wall.

"Your card goes in one of the slots - it doesn't matter which one. And a door will open for you to enter. Inside is pretty dark and the first few moments are uncomfortable, but before you know it, you're with your Assignment. When you come back, you'll exit through the same door and remove your card from the wall. It won't look the same, it will be grey." Mallory carefully runs her slender fingers over a few of the glass cards that protrude from the wall.

I struggle to imprint every word she just said into my memory but I'm afraid I'll forget something important.

"Are you ready?"

I take a deep breath. "Yes, I think so."

"I'll go first, so you can see what I do…okay?"

I nod and watch as she slides her glass card into one of the available slots. The door to our right slowly opens and Mallory walks confidently toward it. With her hand on the knob, she looks over her shoulder at me a final time and smiles before closing the door.

That's it?

I stare at the wall, looking for the slot I want to use, and as I reach up to slide my glass card into the spot I've picked, the door behind me flies open. Niles stands in the doorway, looking frazzled.

"Niles?"

"Piper! I'm glad I made it before you left!" He takes a deep breath before entering and walks quickly to me. I return his hug and when he steps back he takes another breath before talking.

"I'm really sorry I'm late. I had a New Arrival to accompany to Orientation. I wasn't expecting your fist case to come so soon."

"Niles, it's okay. Mallory showed me what to do." I smile big at him, hoping my face is full of confidence.

"That was very kind of her." He nods approvingly. "I will have to thank her."

"She just left on an assignment. She went first so I could see what to do." I nod at the door she passed through just moments before.

"Well, when she returns then." He gestures to the wall. "Which one will you pick?"

"Oh, I was thinking this one." I raise the glass key up to the wall and slide it into an empty space. Niles grins as he watches and the door to our left opens with a soft whoosh sound.

"What?" I send a curious glance his way.

"That's the portal I used for my first case."

"How do you remember which portals you used?" I'm surprised.

"Piper, I've had many, many cases. More assignments than there are portals. I guess I had my favorites." He smiles until a funny look spreads across his face.

"Do you miss it?" I ask quietly.

"Sometimes, but my job now is equally as fulfilling." He nods at the door, "Okay, it's your turn. I'll be here when you come back."

I walk slowly toward the door and Mallory was right, its pitch black on the other side. I glance at Niles and he is nodding with a smile plastered to his wrinkled face, using his hands to 'shoo' me forward.

"Go ahead. You'll be fine." He says.

I stop at the threshold and give him a final smirk. With my hand on the knob, I hear his voice reassuring me once more.

"Good luck, Piper, I know you will do great."

Trish Marie Dawson

CHAPTER 8

I stand absolutely still, afraid to move, afraid to breathe. With the door closed behind me, I see nothing but blackness. It's eerily quiet other than my own thoughts and I'm on the verge of panicking when I feel a pinching sensation start at my feet and quickly travel up my legs.

What the heck is that?!

I dance on my toes, thinking something is crawling on me in the dark. The pinching sensation moves over my hips and around my stomach. I gingerly touch my midsection with only my fingertips but there is nothing there, other than my clothing. The pinching works its way up my chest and a strangled sound escapes my mouth as it passes over my throat. By the time it reaches the top of my head, I'm in full-on panic mode.

I want out, let me out of here! I scream hysterically into the darkness and then suddenly the pinching stops.

Oh, thank you, thank you, THANK YOU!

I feel...light. Suspended, maybe? I try moving but I have no sensation in my limbs. *This is strange. Is this what being paralyzed feels like?* I can't see anything and it's still very dark and quiet. No, wait...I *do* hear something. *Snoring? Is that someone snoring?* Great. My first Assignment is asleep - which means I'm stuck in the darkness for who knows how long.

If I had fingers, I'd be twiddling them. If I had toes, I'd be tapping my foot impatiently. But seeming that it's really just my awareness that is present, I have to wait.

How irritating. The time moves slowly but eventually the snoring stops. A peek of light floods around me before it's gone almost instantly.

Come on, wake up. Brightness encompasses me once more and a few seconds pass by before it is gone this time.

Wake up, sleepy-head.

This time, the glow of light stays put and I see through my Assignment clearly. I struggle to process what's right in front of me...is it, yes...it's a pillow...inside a burgundy-colored case, and beyond that is a starkly furnished bedroom. I sense my Assignment stretch and I look up at the dingy popcorn ceiling and the body I'm inhabiting rolls over. The room is small, not much bigger than a walk-in closet. I'm antsy for my Assignment to start the day...I really want to know what her name is so I can stop calling her my *'Assignment'*.

The room comes into better focus as she sits up and stretches again. I wait patiently, eager for the trip to the bathroom where I'll see her face for the first time. The room tilts as my Assignment gazes to the left where there is a small table beside the bed with dark water rings stained into the wood. I scowl.

Ever heard of a coaster?

A cell phone sits next to a metal bedside lamp, its red light blinking furiously. It must need to be charged. We walk across the room which takes about one second...it's a seriously small space. A door stands open and beyond it I see a toilet.

Yay! Where's the mirror?! As we get closer I see how badly the toilet needs to be cleaned. *Eww. That's just nasty.* I don't get a glimpse in the mirror right away and if I had my lips, I'd pout.

Then something strange and unexpected happens. Instead of my Assignment sitting down on the toilet, she stands - to *pee.* And that's when I realize a mistake was made.

I'm in a man?! Oh no, someone is in deep trouble back at the Station. I wish my arms were still around so I could cross them stubbornly at my chest in disdain. *You've GOT to be kidding me.*

How is this going to work? Somewhere, my foot is tapping with irritation. I wasn't expecting this and I surely wasn't prepared for my first case to be a guy. For *any* of my cases to be guys, actually.

Eventually the toilet flushes...after what seems like an hour of urinating. *I mean seriously, how much can a male bladder hold?!* As the mirror comes into view I want to close my eyes, because I'm afraid of what I'm about to see. But since I can't close what I don't have, I'm forced to stare at the mirror when his head lifts up.

The sleepy face of the most beautiful boy I've ever seen greets me. *This could be bad, really bad.* The last time I thought anyone was this cute, I learned the hard way that cute doesn't mean nice. I play my Trainer's voice through my head...trying to remember all the scenarios that were placed before me to prepare me for this moment. I'm completely blank.

He runs his hand along his chiseled jaw, which is full of dark morning stubble. I don't know what to think but I'm sure if I had my mouth, I'd be gawking. His lips are full and luscious from sleep and his hooded eyelids blink at his reflection slowly. I notice, as well as feel, the sadness from his expression. The bloodshot white of his eyes clash against the blue of his irises and I think he's either very tired, or hung-over...*maybe both?*

I watch, unable to blink – even if I had the ability to do so, as he runs his hand through the soft, dark curls of his jet-black hair and they bounce gently down onto his forehead. He can't be younger than me, so I assume he must be nineteen...the cap for my Assignment age limit.

As he brushes his teeth, too quickly, I think...I get glimpses of his chest and biceps. He's not overly large, but is in obviously great shape. I guess he's about six feet tall. My sordid past all but fades away as I visually absorb this man from head to toe. I guess my teenage hormones aren't forever broken after-all. No longer upset with the mix-up, I think to myself that I will have to thank the person who gave me this case…because despite the brick wall I've built around myself, I realize this man just might be perfect.

♡

It takes him ridiculously long to get out of the tiny apartment he apparently lives in alone. Once we are outside, I drink in the fresh air – *I think I can actually smell it!* And when my Assignment hops onto a bike for a ride across town I revel in the feeling of the air on his skin. He didn't wear a helmet though and I nag him over an entire city block for it. I hope he hears me.

We ride up and down some seriously hilly streets as I wonder where we are. It's a place I've never been to, but it's lovely. We pass block after block of tall Italianate and American Stick style row houses and I instantly fall in love with each neighborhood. The protruding bay windows are my favorite and I imagine some pretty great window seats inside the buildings.

We come to the top of a hill and the view on the other side takes my breath away. I'm looking at the Golden Gate Bridge not far off into the distance!

No way! I'm in San Francisco!

As the bike starts to fly dangerously fast down the other side of the massive hill, I remember this sensation…one of carelessness and feeling indestructible and I snap rather indecorously out of my architecture reverie to yell for the first time at my Assignment.

Slow down, or you're going to kill yourself!

The bike continues at break-neck speed down the hill, dodging around the few vehicles on the narrow road. I suck in a deep breath and scream so loud I'm sure wherever my ears are, they are ringing in protest.

SLOW DOWN, NOW!

I feel the tug of gravity against us as the bike brakes are applied.

That's better.

I wish I had my butt so I could collapse into a chair with relief. Instead, I see us cross over a set of trolley tracks and a man at a magazine stand whistles a hello in our direction. My Assignment releases the handlebars and waves an arm at him in response.

Keep both hands on the handlebars!

He ignores me and sets his free hand loosely on his thigh and somewhere my mouth pouts in unabashed aggravation. He is not making our first day easy on me.

When he finally stops and locks his bike up in front of a small but posh looking coffee shop, I will myself to relax. Surely we are safer with caffeine than his two wheeled horror-ride. He glides into the shop and I say *glide* because his lithe and graceful body does just that, and instead of stopping at the counter to order, he pushes through the waist-high swing door and we disappear into the moderately small bowels of the shop.

with his head on the back of the sofa and his hand casually tucked down the front of his shorts, I find it.

Holy crap.

Trish Marie Dawson

CHAPTER 9

I so badly want to forget what I've seen through Sloan's memories. I want to cry for him, hug him and make it all disappear. I think of Mallory and wonder if this is how it was for her when she became my Volunteer. I want to shudder, hug my knees and rock back and forth on the ground like a scared toddler.

And I thought I *had problems. Poor Sloan.*

I don't even know how to begin processing the information I've collected from him, so I start at the beginning. When he was four his uncle began molesting him. It lasted until he was nine, when his mother remarried and the blended family moved from Cleveland to San Francisco.

Years of being the third caregiver for his mildly Autistic step-brother changed Sloan from an imaginative, creative yet often times shy boy into a nervous and quiet recluse. And then he turned sixteen, started learning how to drive a car and with the few bouts of freedom he was able to get, he had just started coming out of his shell before the accident happened.

On a rainy day, he came down the hill near their townhome too fast and the slick road caused the car to slide out of control. Playing in the tiny front yard, dressed in a yellow slicker with green frogs, was Mick, his younger step-brother. Sloan couldn't stop and the front of the car catapulted over the driveway column and crashed down violently into the front yard…right on top of Mick, crushing him. Sloan's mother saw it all happen from the kitchen window. It took Mick three very painful days to die in the hospital.

Less than a year later, his step-father left his mother and her drinking addiction passed down to Sloan. Three weeks ago his mother died of alcohol poisoning. Sloan didn't go to the small funeral; he was drunk in a bar down the street from his apartment, making out with one of the big-busted servers. He's had over twenty sexual partners in the last year but a few weeks ago he had an STD scare and thankfully he's kept his pants on for the most part since then.

Crap. This is a lot for my first case. Can I do this?

As I push further into his thoughts, I find the purpose for me being here. It's the loaded .45 that he keeps hidden in the shoebox at the top of his closet. He bought it the day before yesterday, off a street punk for $50. *That's how he plans on doing it…shooting himself?* It seems graphic but I learned in my training that more men than women choose a gun for suicide…it's more efficient.

Oh, Sloan. How do I bring you back from here?

He sighs in his sleep and I know he's dreaming of Mick…and his goofy smile.

♥

I urge Sloan awake as soon as I feel see the soft glow of the sun as it makes its sleepy appearance on the horizon behind his closed lids. I have an idea on how to start his day differently than yesterday, but I'll need his help.

Wake up, sleepy head. It's time to start a new day!

When that doesn't work, I tap the ghost of my foot impatiently and chew on my missing lip. *Hmm.* Perhaps something with a bit more volume is needed?

FIRE! FIRE! FIRE! THERE'S A FIRE! GET UP!

Sloan's eyes fly open and finally I'm let out of the darkness.

"What the hell?" Sloan scrambles to his feet, patting at his chest and spinning around the room wildly. "What's burning?"

I love the husky sound of his early-morning voice. And I laugh deliciously that my warning was heard, though I know it's a rude way to wake someone up.

Go take your thirty minute pee break and throw on your workout clothes, you are going for a run.

At first I don't think it will work, but since he's obviously wide awake thanks to my *FIRE! FIRE! FIRE!* joke, he stumbles around the saggy sofa, through the bedroom and ends up in the bathroom. *Yes, for small victories!*

I wait as patiently as I can while he does his morning duties in the bathroom and I praise him when he takes five extra seconds brushing his teeth. He grumbles when he stands in front of his dresser. I know he is seriously considering my plea to go for a run and I want to jump up and down like a caveman, but alas, I have no legs. So I do what any girl would do, I help him pick the right outfit.

Dressed in dark blue workout shorts, a tight white t-shirt that hugs his muscles perfectly and a 49ers ball cap, he stops in the kitchen long enough to gulp down an eight ounce cup of water...at my constant insistence. *I think I'm getting the hang of this!* He pops the ear buds of his iPod in as he jogs casually down the stairs and I squeal in delight as Foster the People's *Pumped Up Kicks* blares loudly into his ears. *Oh, music, how I have missed you!*

See, Sloan. I told you this was going to be a better day.

I feel invigorated when we return to his apartment an hour later. Sloan is hungry and very sweaty...which doesn't bother me at all as I catch glimpses of his form stuck to his damp clothing. But as he peels out of his outfit to jump into the warm shower I almost wish I have hands to cover my eyes. Thankfully he spends most of the time with his head under the warm stream, which means his eyes are closed. I think of all the times I showered, or bathed, after Ryan Burke and that Mallory was right there with me. *Ick.* It's sort of pervy, when I really think about it. No amount of female hormones has me excited to be alone in a shower with a ridiculously good looking young man. Not yet.

After he wraps a large and frayed towel around his narrow hips, he saunters into the kitchen to open the fridge. There's nothing inside except for a moldy piece of cheese, barely an ounce left on the bottom of a Sunny-D jug and a bowl of partially dehydrated Jell-O.

Oh good lord, get dressed and go to the grocery store. He reaches for the cheese and actually sniffs it before I snap at him: *Grocery store, NOW!*

He glides through his apartment and stands in front of his old and surprisingly cool distressed dresser again, rubbing the stubble on his chin. *And I thought girls had a hard time picking out clothes.* After helping him decide on a pair of jeans and a fashionably frayed *Coca-Cola* shirt, he pulls on his shoes and tugs on his 49ers cap again. I try to tell him that's gross…considering he put the sweaty hat on top of clean hair, but he ignores me.

You're going to have awful hat-hair, just watch.

To my dismay, instead of hailing a cab, he unchains his horror-on-wheels from the courtyard bike locker and we pedal smoothly out onto the San Francisco streets. Today is different though, I sense a change in his riding. He's not rushed at all and seems to be enjoying taking his time biking through the neighborhood. This gives me a chance to leisurely look up at the Queen Anne row houses in his neck of the woods. How come I never visited this city? It's not that far away from San Diego. *Maybe because you were only eighteen when you died?* Sadness washes over me quickly and thoughts of my Father and Bree flood my mind. Aware that I am violating one of the major Assignment rules, which is to 'never, ever, make things about YOU', I struggle to turn my thoughts away from my past and stare through his eyes at the day around him.

Food, finally! I don't think he knows what to do with half the stuff he brought home, because I nearly lost my voice shouting out the names of colorful vegetables and fruits and whole grains in the store. It was an almost painful challenge to keep him from the candy and frozen food sections.

He sets the bags on the counter and starts unpacking them slowly. When he pulls the pineapple out, the largest thing I *MADE* him buy, he stares at it with wonder, before setting it carefully back down on the counter-top; as if he's afraid it might come to life and tear his hand off if he jostles it. It's a golden color and I had him sniff it in the store, with some coaxing of course…to make sure it was ripe.

I sit my imaginary butt down on an imaginary velvet throne and put my feet up on an imaginary footstool made of rubies and gold as he moves easily about the kitchen, putting food away, and pondering what to actually eat. I feel like a Goddess. I *rock* this job!

He stands with his hands comically on his hips. "What the hell will I do with you?" He's staring down the pineapple, possibly challenging it to a duel. Eventually, he grumbles, "I don't know why I bought that."

Because you're going to cut it up and toss it in with some chopped apples and mandarin oranges...dump it on some of that plain yogurt and crumble that yummy looking granola on top. And it's going to be sooo yummy!

"I guess I could make a fruit salad." He says quietly.

That's what I just said!

"Or order pizza."

He moves toward the greasy flyer stuck on the fridge by a rusty bottle opener magnet and my imaginary footstool disappears, as does my imaginary throne, and I fall flat on my imaginary butt.

What?! NO!

He slumps up against the fridge in frustration. I know he can hear me, so I dive in once again.

You are NOT ordering greasy junk food, no matter how wonderful it tastes, because you worked out today...and it made you feel good. And you want to feel good. MAKE THE DAMN FRUIT SALAD!

"Okay, fine!" He yells at the empty room.

Did he *actually* hear me? I wonder if all assignments talk to themselves as much as he talks back to me. It's something I have to remember to ask Niles about the instant I return to the Station.

My throne returns as he butchers the pineapple badly but eventually it's cut into edible bites. I watch him toss it in with the rest of the fruit. Almost as an afterthought he pulls the yogurt out of the fridge and the granola from the cupboard and combines it all into one very messy bowl.

Excellent job. I say, and I mean it.

He's asleep in front of the TV again. He has awful sleeping habits...I'll have to work on that. Since he has to be at *Steam* by nine the next morning, I doubt he'll want to get up early again for a run but I plan on trying anyway. In order for him to improve he has to break his bad habits first. He has to learn to care about himself again – inside and out. *It's possible, Volunteers do this every day*, I remind myself. Sloan seems like a tough case though. And not for the first time I wonder why anyone at the Station would think he was a good match for *me*. I doubt I will ever understand the politics of my new existence.

I'm dawdling on that idea when Sloan's cell rings. It's sitting on the coffee table, just beside his propped up feet. He doesn't move on the first ring, or even the second, but he stirs on the third and sits up to grab the phone by the fourth.

"What?" He answers it without reading the caller ID.

"Sloan Nash. Are you ignoring me for a reason?" A syrupy voice teases him from the other side of the phone.

"Jess?" His feet fly off the table and he leans forward on the couch, rubbing his hand through his hair briskly to wake himself up.

"Were you expecting someone else to call this late, baby?"

She's still teasing him. Judging her voice alone, I bet she's beautiful…tall perhaps, thin of course, big breasted, tiny waist, long and perfect hair, orthodontist-made teeth. I instantly hate her.

"Nah. Just been busy, you know. Work." *Is he dodging her? Miss Fake-Boobs Perfect Hair Ortho-Teeth with the should be illegal sexy voice girl?*

"You don't return my calls." She sounds as if she's fake pouting. *Uhg.*

"Sorry," he replies flatly, with no emotion.

"Are you busy tonight, baby? Want some company?"

"Umm."

What?! You can't be considering this, Sloan…it's almost one in the morning!

"Sorry, Jess. It's late and I work tomorrow…you know, first thing."

Phew. No doubt you dodged a nearly fatal bullet there.

"You sure, baby?" She sounds ridiculous.What woman throws herself at a man in the middle of the night, when he's clearly not interested? *Is she drunk? She must be drunk.*

"Have you been drinking?" Sloan asks her.

The silence on the other end is enough to make me want to giggle. She IS drunk and clearly embarrassed to be caught. I listen to their awkward goodbyes and urge Sloan to bed. He flips the TV off and grumbles the whole five feet into his room, but he's asleep almost as soon as his head hits the pillow.

Oh, Sloan. We'll work on your laundry list of problems in the morning. Until then, sleep well. I have work to do in here.

CHAPTER 10

It's dawn again and my gentle urges to wake him up aren't working, so I belt out Katy Perry's *Part Of Me* until I hear Sloan's half-conscious voice mumbling in protest.

"Oh my god, turn it down."

I sing louder until he opens his eyes. *Yay – light!* I stop singing but laugh when I hear Sloan humming the song on his way to the bathroom. For the whole ten minutes we are in there, I attempt to pump him up for a quick early morning run and he surprises me by not being mentally combative.

We are back in the apartment half an hour later, sweat soaking through the front and back of Sloan's shirt. He peels off his clothes as he walks across the living room and I sense he's about to dump them onto the floor.

HAMPER!

He balls up his shorts and t-shirt and jumps high into the air to toss them into the packed hamper in the corner of his room as if they are a basketball.

Hmm...tonight when you get off of work, we are going to do some laundry AND put the clothes back into your dresser.

I've seen enough of his body by now to be comfortable with it in naked form from the chest down, but every time he's facing the mirror I'm surprised with his looks. I don't sense from him that he enjoys being attractive, or is even aware of it for that matter. In fact, his self-esteem is very low.

One thing at a time, we can work on your feelings of self-loathing tomorrow.

♀

The brown-haired woman from Friday isn't working today and I'm grateful for some reason. The day goes by quickly thanks to the busy Sunday crowd and the only part of the day I've had to yell at Sloan was on the bike rides to and from work. I appreciate each good decision he makes on his own and make a point to pump him full of praise when the moment calls for it. But back in the apartment, it's just him alone with me...except he doesn't know I'm here.

What will you make for dinner?

He searches through the groceries we purchased the day before but there aren't too many options; it's hard to ride a bike and carry bags at the same time, so he didn't buy too much. He settles on grilled veggies with rice stuffed into some pita bread and a side of left-over fruit salad. I know he really likes the fruit concoction and it makes me deliriously happy.

Just before he shoves the pita full of rice and veggies into his mouth I get an idea.

How about some music, Sloan?

His hand actually hovers in front of his mouth and for a brief moment I believe he's heard me, but then the food goes in and he takes a massive bite, spilling grains of rice onto his plate. I would pout if physically possible but my suddenly dour mood is lifted when he pushes himself up from the couch, still chewing his food and walks across the room to turn on his radio. *Punching In A Dream* is just ending and I tap my missing hands on my missing knees. I *love* this song.

After dinner Sloan washes his dishes and though I encourage him to wipe them off and put them away, he leaves them out to air dry on a large hand towel instead. So I move on to the next chore. It takes a half hour of my nagging to convince him to do laundry but eventually he caves and drops his nearly full bottle of laundry soap on the top of the heaping hamper with obvious displeasure.

The laundry room is a short walk downstairs and across the courtyard. Thankfully it's empty when he enters, because there are only two sets of machines. He over-loads one of the washers and doesn't bother to separate the colors and I try hard not to complain...he *IS* doing his laundry after-all. Plus, he has his iPod going, so I get to lose myself in music while he works.

Just as Sloan slams the washer lid down, a woman in her thirties comes into the small room and thumps her laundry basket onto the counter. A young boy about five years old is entwined around her legs, obviously shy around Sloan.

"Are you using both machines?" She asks him with a smile.

"Oh, no. This one's free."

He gestures to the empty washer and steps aside so she can dump her clothes into it. The boy is still wrapped tightly around her legs but sends a quick smirk in Sloan's direction. I feel a stirring in him as he watches the pair.

"Thanks!" She says before leaving the room as her boy runs ahead of her into the corner of the courtyard. A plastic truck is waiting for him in the dirt border of a flower bed.

Sloan watches them through the window for a few minutes and I know he is thinking about his mother. He misses her but he's also very angry with her still. She abandoned him in a sense, left him when he needed her most.

No wonder you have no functional female relationships.

He snorts, as if thinking of something funny but I can't catch what it is. Eventually he turns away from the window with the view of the Mom who is sitting near her son as he plays with his dump truck...carefully maneuvering around the planted Gerbera Daisies so as not to disturb them. Sloan finds an old magazine to flip through and when the buzzer on the washer goes off, he hops down from the counter and tosses his clothes into the dryer.

It will be at least an hour before they are dry, so we head back up the stairs to the second floor of the complex. Of course Sloan plops down onto the couch and turns on the TV. I wait until he's completely engrossed in a restaurant makeover show before I start my borage of questions.

Who are your friends?

What are your passions?

Can you ever forgive yourself for Mick's death?

Why the gun, Sloan?

I wait patiently as his mind ponders through the answers slowly. Friends...he trusts no one. Very Mulder of him, but I get it. Passions – that's difficult...he remembers taking guitar classes when he was younger but after Mick...well, everything sort of stopped after the accident. Other than random sex with strangers, he hasn't had much of a passion in years. But he likes nature, he likes being outdoors...which is why he doesn't mind using the bike as his main form of transportation. His mind skims directly over the topic of forgiveness without pause. The gun...he spends a considerable amount of time pondering this question. I've heard the same commercial for toilet bowl cleaner three times before he's done.

You need to get rid of the gun, Sloan.

"No, not yet."

If you keep it, you won't heal. You have to let it go.

"There's nothing to let go of. No one needs me here."

And there it is. The real reason...he feels abandoned, needed by no one...*alone.*

That's not true. I'm sure it's not.

"There's nothing for me here. No one."

You have me, I'm here with you.

He drags his shaky hands down his face and sighs heavily. "This talking to yourself thing has gotta stop, Sloan," he says with an empty laugh.

You don't have to talk back, just listen.

He pounds his fists into his temple twice and I know he's done for the night. I quiet and let his mind wander once again to the TV.

It's okay. There's no rush.

By the time he heads back downstairs to retrieve his clothes, I'm lost in thought. This is hard. Trying to pick a pathway to steer him onto without completely taking away his free-will is almost impossible. But then I remember the box he has buried in the back of his closet and I get an idea. It might not work, in fact it might back-fire, but I think the risk is worth it, because he also has a gun in that closet.

♡

The daylight has completely faded from the sky, leaving only the light-post on the sidewalk as illumination outside Sloan's bedroom window. The bedside lamp showers a yellow glow across half of the room, creating dark shadows in every corner. He's standing at the foot of the bed, chewing on his lower lip, eyeing the box warily. I so badly want him to open it so I can see exactly what's inside but if I push too hard he might walk away completely, so I wait…quietly.

The cardboard is old and the tape that no longer sticks to the lid is faded. It looks as if he's opened the box many times over the years but it's been awhile. I can tell by the rising level of his anxiety.

He blows out a huge gust of air and sits down on the bed, next to the box. It's a perfect square, maybe two feet on each side, the same amount deep. He reaches for the lid and his hand stills just inches away. I don't think he's going to touch it after all but then he flicks the lid off in a flurry, grazing the top with only his fingertips.

Inside is a large plastic *Darth Vader* figure, several matchbox cars, a baseball tucked inside a youth's baseball cap, several postcards of wild animals from the San Diego Zoo gift shop, and a small *Bumblebee* toy…in car form. There are photo albums at the bottom of the box and some paperwork, as well as messy finger paintings and drawings that Mitch and Sloan did together.

You can do this Sloan.

He reaches slowly into the box and pulls out each of the toys. He doesn't touch the ball or cap. But he lays the *Vader, Bumblebee* and small metal cars out on the bed. After fingering each of them lovingly, he scoops them up using the bottom of his t-shirt like a hammock and heads for the front door.

In less than five minutes we are downstairs and across the courtyard standing in front of Laundry Mom's apartment. Sloan is so nervous, I think he's sweating. When she answers the door she is wearing pajama shorts and a loose fitting sleep shirt, obviously no bra, and I think she's embarrassed that it's him on the other side of the screen, judging from the rising color in her cheeks. Her son is somewhere in the back of the apartment, playing loudly with a toy that screeches like a siren. *How does this not drive her crazy?!*

"Hi." She glances at his midsection, curious about the bulge in his shirt. But she's not afraid...*good.*

"Um, hi. I'm Sloan, I live upstairs...uh, we met earlier in the laundry room." He's trying to smile...he is so nervous.

She laughs and her short blonde hair bounces on her shoulders as she nods at him. "Yes, I remember. What can I do for you, Sloan?"

"Oh. Well," he opens up the front of his shirt to show her the toys through the screen. She raises an eyebrow at him, confused, and both Sloan and Laundry Mom jump when her son squeals behind her legs. He's peeking at Sloan from between her knees.

"Are those for me!" It's not quite a question, more an excited declaration and Sloan grins down at him.

"Well, yes...if it's alright with your mom." He looks up at her, to see her smiling.

"Are those really for him?" She says with a laugh as she struggles to keep her young son from scrambling out the flimsy screen door. Eventually she stoops to lift him and props him expertly on her hip.

"Yeah, they used to belong to...well, I don't need them anymore." Sloan is at a loss for words.

Laundry Mom can't hold onto her squirming boy anymore and she opens the screen, freeing him from her arms at the same time. I notice her ring finger is bare. *Single mom?* Sloan squats down and opens his shirt up once again to show the curious boy the small collection of cars. He's most interested in the *Bumblebee* toy and that's the first thing he snatches and drags across the ground. Sloan watches him with child-like wonder. I know it's been a very, very long time since he's seen these toys played with.

Deep breath, Sloan. You're okay, it's all good. He loves them, see?

Sloan nods slowly and stands so that Laundry Mom can gather the rest of the toys from his shirt. Her blush deepens when she catches a glimpse of his exposed abdomen and I'm sure she's enjoying how low his jeans hang on his narrow and defined hips.

"Wow, thanks," she says.

"No problem. They were just sitting in my closet. Figure your boy here can have some fun with them."

"Oh, he will…I promise," she laughs softly.

"Okay then, see you around." Sloan backs away from the door and steps carefully around the boy, who is happily turning *Bumblebee* around in circles on the WIPE YOUR PAWS mat.

"Sure…on laundry days." She winks at him, and I think she's flirting.

Whoa now, calm down Mrs. Cougar. He's at least fifteen years your junior!

Sloan laughs and reaches down to ruffle the small boy's hair. The child looks up at him briefly and stutters out a happy thanks when prompted by his mother.

As we walk back to the apartment I feel something different inside Sloan…a lightness of sorts. I am sure it's a good thing, so I praise him for being strong enough to go through Mick's box and for being brave enough to finally let some of him go.

After Sloan climbs into bed, he tosses and turns for almost an hour before falling asleep. I wish I could sleep too when the darkness surrounds me, but I know there's more work to do. Sloan has made a lot of progress but he's nowhere near clear of danger. Not with that gun around.

CHAPTER 11

It takes just over a week for Sloan to get into the habit of running every morning without my nagging him first thing at dawn. It takes another week for him to consistently put his dirty clothes into the hamper and not use the floor. I've been on assignment with Sloan for almost three weeks and he feels lighter, not as weighed down by his sadness.

Today is his day off and instead of turning on the TV and parking himself on the couch with a giant box of delivery pizza across his lap, he's cleaning the apartment. Amazingly, this is not my doing. He has a date. Well, sort of.

Laundry Mom turned cougar is coming over with her son Gabe for dinner. It wasn't exactly what I was expecting when I spent three days urging him to invite a friend over to hang out. I don't really like the flirty looks the single mom gives Sloan but she's a person he's willing to make his friend. And this is a good thing.

If I knew you'd actually clean your apartment for a guest, I would have tried to get you to throw a party weeks ago.

I help him pick out seasonings for the spaghetti sauce and remind him when it's time to pull the garlic bread from the oven. Living with only my Dad for a few years definitely made me more of a foodie. I wish I had appreciated that back then. *Enough...not about you, remember Piper?* I turn my thoughts away from home and back to dinner.

When a soft knock on the door is followed by a flurry of shorter knocks below the door knob, Sloan is sliding the rest of the chopped veggies off the cutting board and into the bowl of lettuce.

"Just a sec!" He hollers across the small apartment. It smells of lemon *Pine-Sol* and Italian food. I wish I could taste it. *I do miss good food.*

He wipes his hands on a towel and throws it over his shoulder with a flick of his wrist. I catch his reflection on the glass front of the microwave as he walks by. His smile would send shivers down my spine, if it was connected to me still. The hand towel looks as if it's always been at home, draped over the top of his upper body...he's getting more confidant in the kitchen, it suits him.

See that - you look like a bona-fide chef now!

"Hi." He smiles politely as he opens the door and invites the expectant duo in.

Gabe grabs at his legs momentarily for a quick hug before running around the small living area, finally settling on the couch with his *Darth Vader* and *Bumblebee* toys. I can see bulges on both sides of his jeans and assume he has also stashed some of the matchbox cars into his pockets. He really is a cute kid.

"I brought some dessert wine. I didn't know if you like white or red."

Cougar Mom hands him the bottle of chilled Moscato and he smiles at her while he carries it into the kitchen. I feel stirrings inside him as he lets his mind wander. He's actually imagining her without her clothes on! It's even easy for me to do, since she's wearing a very short summer skirt with a gauzy sleeveless top. The outline of her baby-blue bra is clearly defined. This is NOT what you wear to a friendly-neighbor dinner.

Easy boy. It's just food. With a friend, remember?

"Thanks, Sandy."

He smiles at her again, I can tell because she bats her eyelashes at him in response. *Yes, I know his smiles are ridiculously sexy, but get over it woman, he's too young for you!* I scowl inwardly. I'm tapping my missing foot irritably and somewhere my after-life eyes are batting in mocked exaggeration at her.

I wish I had a dark corner to hide in while they eat dinner. The conversation is electric with sexual undertones from both of them. Sloan ignores my complaints and warnings completely, so I have no choice but to watch silently as the playful banter between the two unfold.

I know it's been a while, Sloan. But come on. She's almost old enough to be your mom!

Gabe adores Sloan and spends half the meal trying to climb into his lap. At first Sloan seems surprised by the close contact, but he's really rather good with children…and somehow he's able to get the boy to eat at least a third of his meal, including three pieces of lettuce and a tomato wedge.

When Gabe saunters away from the table to sit on the couch for a late evening viewing of *SpongeBob,* Sandy makes her first move. It's a subtle gesture but it ripples through Sloan like a jolt of lightening. I can almost smell the charred remnants of my imaginary hair as my head bursts into flame somewhere far away from here.

He is staring down at his lap, where her petite hand is resting just inside the top of his thigh while she laughs, in the middle of some story I lost interest in nearly half an hour ago. Back at the Station, my mouth gapes at her. I feel Sloan's heart-rate increase dramatically and that stirring sensation roars through him like the Grand Rapids.

"And so I told him he couldn't possibly expect me to carry that table out to the car *myself,* and wouldn't you know, it took three men to get it into my little Explorer." She laughs and I'm bored out of my mind listening to her talk about furniture shopping for her apartment.

Sloan laughs along with her, though I doubt he is interested in the story either. If he's remembered any of it at all. He's currently preoccupied with

Sandy's sheer top. Her small breasts sit up a bit too high and I assume it's mostly padding making her look that perky. I almost *want* him to strip her clothes off so he can be disappointed by her lack of real breasts.

"Want more wine?" As he stands her hand slowly slides off his leg.

"Sure," she purrs.

"How did you like dinner?" He is now in the kitchen, refilling her wine glass. I notice he doesn't top off his own.

Smart choice, Sloan.

"Oh, Sloan, it was great! You're such a tease!" She has turned in the chair to face him and he watches as she slowly uncrosses, then re-crosses her legs.

"A tease?" He balks at her in surprise…we both do actually. Neither of us having missed her Sharon Stone moment.

"You said you couldn't cook! And this was magnificent. Thank you."

"Oh, you're welcome. It wasn't as hard as I thought it would be." He laughs.

That's because I was helping you, dork.

I try to zone out as they begin cleaning up the table and putting away the leftover food. There's so much intentional elbow bumping, arm grazing, and hand brushing at the kitchen sink I want to puke. It's the first time I have EVER actually *wanted* to throw up.

The kiss is unexpected. He's leaning forward one moment, sliding the clean plates into the cupboard and when he turns, her mouth is just *there*. A burst of tiny firecrackers seem to go off inside him. I feel lighter suddenly, almost untethered to him. I don't understand the sensation and it freaks me out.

What the heck is that?!

I panic and begin screaming in his head. *YOU CANNOT MAKEOUT WITH THIS WOMAN WHILE HER SON SLEEPS ON YOUR COUCH!*

He pulls away from her instantly and she looks up at him with large golden-brown eyes, surprised and maybe – *hopefully* - even shocked by his sudden withdraw.

That's right, lady! Back off!

"Sorry…but…what about Gabe?" He looks over his shoulder to glance at the couch.

As the heat inside him slowly cools, I try to stop myself from mentally hyperventilating.

"Oh, gosh. You're right."

She smiles awkwardly before walking over to the couch to check on her sleeping child. Sloan follows her and I feel him warm up inside as he watches the rhythmic rise and fall of Gabe's chest while he dreams.

"It's late. I should probably take him home." She stares at Sloan for a moment too long, waiting for a protest, maybe?

Send her home, Sloan.

"Can I help you?" He asks, gesturing to Gabe.

"No, I carry him all the time." She smiles before tilting upward and planting a soft kiss on Sloan's cheek…her fingers caress the muscles of his biceps while she slowly pulls away. "This was really nice. Maybe next time we can do it at my place, since Gabe has his own room."

Her implication is not lost on either of us. I'm fuming.

"Okay, sure." He agrees a bit too eagerly and then walks them to the door…Sandy with her arms full of Gabe's sleeping body, and Sloan, softly chewing on his lower lip.

"Thanks, again. I had a great night."

"Me too." His answer is short and simple, but his voice is husky with emotion.

Oh crap. I think he really likes her. Even though I know it's very wrong, I can't help but feel a fiery pang of jealously slice through me. It's like a dagger to my heart. I try hard to push this feeling aside. I should be encouraging new relationships, not hoping to keep Sloan all to myself. It's *not* appropriate, I know this.

Sandy smiles broadly, before turning to walk down the open hall to the concrete-step staircase, her shoulder-length hair swaying like a pendulum against the back of her neck. Sloan leans against the doorway, gazing down at them as she slowly crosses the courtyard. She turns to see him watching just before she opens her door and gives him a little wave. He raises his hand up briefly in return and walks back inside the apartment, closing the door behind him softly.

"Huh." He says it out-loud to the empty room.

I imagine my hands on my hips with a stern look of displeasure on my face as Sloan makes his way to the bathroom before undressing and crawling into bed. After he collapses onto his pillow he stares up at the ceiling for a while, gently caressing his lower lip with his index finger, lost in his thoughts about Sandy.

Oh, you just wait till you go to sleep. I'm going to scream so much sense into your brain tonight - even your dreams will be nagging you!

❣

Though I have prepared a plethora of selfish observations laced with an extensive collection of colorful expletives to dish out to him, along with a heaping side of negative comments and a dollop of chiding remarks as the cherry on top of my planned tongue lashing, I fume silently in his head while he snores.

Just in the few weeks that Sloan has been my Assignment, I've grown quite attached to him. I understand completely why Mallory felt let down when I ended things the way I did. She must have worked so hard – *months* – just to have me quit on everything. I refuse to let that happen with Sloan and to my heart-felt delight, he's making tremendous improvements. He hasn't thought of the gun in days. He's learning to take care of his body – internally and externally, which makes him happy. He's making friends too; even if they happen to be older, sex-crazed, single-moms.

Sandy isn't really that bad, is she? I struggle to answer this question, because my first instinct is to say: *YES! She's a HOOCH!* But I know this is ridiculous. She's simply interested sexually in Sloan, and I can't blame her for that. He's gorgeous and on top of that; loves her kid. He'd never hurt her. But she doesn't understand, not even a teeny bit, how messed up Sloan is. I know it all, and I don't think she can handle it. I wonder if anyone really could. It would have to be the perfect woman. Perfect.

I hope you find her, the girl of your dreams…because if anyone deserves to be happy, it's you, Sloan.

I save my near deluge of reprimanding for another time. Tonight, I'll let him sleep in peace. Plus, I have to make a plan for the next few weeks. I can feel the darkness in Sloan ebbing away, and my grasp on him is slipping. I can tell now that our connection isn't as strong. I'm not sure how his case will close but I know I want to leave him with the best possible future I can. I won't fail him.

Trish Marie Dawson

CHAPTER 12

The wet pavement sparkles like glitter while the sun beats down on it after the second downpour of the week. I never imagined a city could look so beautiful after a rainstorm but the hills of San Francisco shine and shimmer like something ethereal. Sloan takes the streets a bit slower now, enjoying his bike rides, but also more aware of the dangers of speeding recklessly. He's starting to come around to the idea that he *may* not want to die just yet.

We pass the familiar corner with the magazine stand and José waves at Sloan from behind the cover of a Spanish *People* magazine. Sloan waves back of course and not long after we are pulling up in front of *Steam*. I'm so familiar with the job by now that I'm certain I could be a master Barista back at the Station...if they had espresso there. I'm sure I can even do the little latte flower art with my eyes closed...that's how confidant I am.

The ladies of the neighborhood (and some that I'm sure don't live anywhere nearby) flock to the shop like crack is slipped into the coffee by the tablespoon. Sloan is much more relaxed around the forward women, which is great for him in the long run, but his change in attitude, and his friendlier demeanor clearly gives some of them hope that Sloan might actually call the number they slip to him on the back of their business cards and coffee receipts. And he won't, I know he won't.

I try to tell myself it's not all Sandy's doing…but I'd be lying. They see each other almost every day…having meals together at least twice a week. And this weekend Gabe will be staying with his grandparents. I'm a little freaked out.

Training was supposed to prepare all Volunteers for experiencing sex through their assignments but I truly do not want to go there with Sloan and Sandy. Not only does she annoy me incessantly but I don't think she's right for him, and even though right now he seems a bit happier, it won't last. And then what? What if something happens between them after I'm already gone? I can't stand the thought of Sandy hurting Sloan but it seems inevitable. Of course – he doesn't agree at all. He's on a Sandy high with the perky-fake-boobs and the flirty I-like-to-touch-you-hands. *Bleck.*

I've let my mind wander so much that I'm amazed to see it's less than five minutes till the end of Sloan's shift. *That was the fastest work day ever!* After he hangs up his apron in the back room and tries his best to avoid the small talk from the Barbie twins sitting at a small table in the corner, he hurries out the front toward the rack where he locked up his bike.

A harried-looking man in his forties leans against the nearby light-post with a folded newspaper in his hand. *Who reads those nowadays?* When Sloan reaches down to fumble with the combination lock, the man lowers the paper slowly and stares in our direction. I think I know him from somewhere but I can't quite place the memory. But as soon as Sloan rises and turns to look up the sidewalk, their eyes meet and memories flash flood through me.

Oh no. Not good, this is not good.

"Sloan." The man speaks his name softly, full of emotion.

I wait to see how long it will take for Sloan to bolt away on his bike but when he actually speaks it surprises both me and the man with the wire-rimmed glasses staring at us anxiously.

"Dad?"

Something changes behind the older man's lenses. His eyes seem to warm a bit and it looks as if he might cry. Perhaps he's been waiting to hear someone refer to him with that title for a long time...too long, I imagine.

"Hi, son."

Neither men move, they just stare at each other. Finally the Barbie twins exit the coffee shop and one of them hollers out a goodbye to Sloan, which seems to snap him back to reality. He shuffles nervously on his feet as he carefully leans the bike handlebars against his thigh. *Maybe he's not going to bolt, after all?*

"What are you doing here?" Sloan asks the question with surprise, but not anger.

"Your girlfriend told me where you work and I wanted to see you." He looks nervous, and rolls the newspaper in his hands until the paper threatens to tear.

"My girlfriend?" Sloan is shocked, rightly so…even though I know *exactly* who his step-dad is referring to.

"Sandy, is it? I went to your apartment and I ran into her downstairs. She said you were working…here." He waves at *Steam* but doesn't seem to be judging the little coffee house.

"Oh."

Yeah, let that shock sink in… 'girlfriend'.

"So, what are you doing around here?" Sloan tries not to sound nervous but I know he is. I can feel his heartbeat accelerate to a speed that shouldn't be possible and his breathing is dangerously erratic. He's actually *afraid* of his step-dad. I want to hug him, but I left my arms in the after-life a couple months ago.

Now it's the older man's turn to look concerned. "Should I not have come?" His masculine voice sounds tiny and hurt.

"No…I mean, yes, its fine. I'm just surprised, I guess. It's been a while." Sloan shifts on his feet again.

"Yes, it has. I'm sorry."

Sloan nearly faints at the words. He grips his fingertips into the handlebars so tightly I'm afraid they might snap off like dry twigs. The race between his heart and lungs has ceased and as his heart rate plummets, I'm afraid he's not breathing at all.

Sloan! Crap! Breathe...bend over - stick your head between your knees...something! BREATHE!

His bike tilts to the side suddenly and crashes loudly onto the curb as Sloan leans into his thighs, lowering his head between his legs.

"Sloan! Are you okay?!"

The newspaper falls with a flourish to the concrete and flops open to the sports page, while Step-Dad rushes to Sloan's side and helps him to a bus bench not far from the front door of the coffee house.

"I'm...fine." He sounds shaky, *not* fine to me.

"Good lord, you gave me a scare."

Step-Dad is sitting on the edge of the bench, right next to Sloan, patting his knee reassuringly, and now I know why he's so familiar...he has Mick's eyes and mouth. The only memories Sloan has with his step-father are fleeting, not nearly detailed enough for me to truly know what the man looks like. Plus, the last few years haven't been kind to him. His face looks gaunt and yellowish. He seems to have aged twenty years in just the last few years. I think I'm just as nervous as Sloan.

"I'm okay. Really, just...maybe I need to eat. Are you hungry?" Sloan asks hesitantly, as if prepared to be let down with a familiar rejection.

"Food...that sounds good. Let's get you something to eat." Step-Dad smiles, and there it is again...a little piece of Mick.

♥

The Chinese restaurant that Sloan picks is one he hasn't visited since I've been on his case. The place is small, with rows of dark-pleather benched seating lining the walls and several square tables with wooden chairs filling up the center of the room. Stunning Chinese artwork as tall as a person hangs inside polished wooden frames on the furthest wall, just behind the self-serve buffet counter.

"You still like Chinese?" Sloan asks.

"Yep! Still my favorite." Step-Dad smiles in response.

Oh, now I get it. Sloan never eats Chinese…does it remind him of the family he lost?

We sit down at a booth, against the wall. There are only three other diners in the restaurant since it's barely four o'clock. The men look around the room, taking in the pleasant Asian ambiance. After they place their orders the server returns with tall plastic cups of water and Sloan takes a long sip.

"I know it must be upsetting, me just showing up." Step-Dad says.

Sloan almost chokes down the water, but manages to set the cup on the table calmly.

"Maybe a little."

When the older man's face falls, I'm sure it will shatter to the ground in a million pieces and the server will have to come to the table and sweep Step-Dad's face up off the floor with a broom and dustpan. *Or, maybe they have one of those cool cordless hand vacs.* The image makes me giggle.

Sloan leans forward, concerned, "I just meant, it's a surprise, is all. I mean, you said...you know..." he waves his hand between them.

"I know. I remember. I said I never wanted to see you again." Step-Dad looks like he's in pain. *As you should.* I think.

This time its Sloan's face that falls but the image of his beautiful features in a heap on the floor is NOT funny.

"I should never have said that, Sloan. It wasn't your fault...it was...an accident. Accidents happen." Step-Dad looks down at his partially full water cup and drags his index finger over the condensation, causing a tiny puddle to form at the base of the cup. "It wasn't right, what I said. What I did...leaving you. And your mom." He looks up at Sloan then and I can feel it, the burning hot sensation that roars around inside him...Sloan is crying. *I* want to cry. I also want to launch myself out of Sloan's mind and slap the hell out of this man!

You abandoned him! You left him with his drunk of a mother, when you all needed each other. You left him alone!

Sloan starts to say something but the server arrives at the table and sets three plates in front of them. Spring rolls sit in a tiny mountain at the center of the table, steaming deliciously. I *really* miss food.

For what seems like hours but is probably only ten minutes, they eat awkwardly. Chew-swallow, repeat. And repeat...and repeat. Eventually I can't handle it anymore.

Ask him why he's here...why now? Why tell you these things now?

I feel him shift in his chair. I KNOW he wants to ask these questions himself.

"Why now?" he asks with his mouth partially full of food. Rice noodles, I think.

Step-Dad lays his fork down on his plate with barely a sound. He looks up at Sloan and smiles sweetly, lovingly.

"Son, I'm dying."

Everything crumbles around me...the foundation I helped him build up over the last several weeks shakes, rattles and rolls like an emotional earthquake. *Oh. Crap.*

"What do you mean, you're dying?" Sloan swallows the mouthful of barely chewed noodles in one forceful gulp.

"I have cancer, Sloan. I've had it for a while. I can't do the treatment again; it's just as bad as the disease." He pauses to reach for his cup and his hand is shaking slightly. "My Doctor urged me to see you," he pauses to clear his throat, "to say sorry...and goodbye."

"Are you kidding me?" The anger in Sloan's voice surprises the older man. "You walk out on mom and me, and let her kill herself with booze, now you come back just to say goodbye?"

The tension between them radiates outward like a nuclear cloud and soon other diners begin to stare at our table. The server returns to fill their water glasses and asks if they would like dessert, though neither has finished their heaping plates of food yet. After the short man scurries away after being unpleasantly dismissed, Step-Dad nods slowly, and speaks.

"You have every right to be angry, every right to hate me. I thought I hated you for a long time. But the truth is it could have been me that caused that…accident. It could have been anyone." He risks looking up at Sloan.

I feel the tears coming again. "I'm so sorry." It's barely above a whisper, Sloan's voice. Like a child's.

Step-Dad is nodding. "I know, son. I know. We both miss him."

CHAPTER 13

We spend the rest of the day with Step-Dad. He has a flight to catch late in the evening and the goodbyes are hard for everyone. I'm sure Sloan's tight hugs are going to leave wrinkles in Step-Dad's light-blue linen shirt. I've never seen Sloan affectionate like this. I can tell that their relationship was a good one, before Mick's death.

"I'm glad you came."

"Me too," Step-Dad replies softly.

"Are you sure you don't want me to come visit, you know…later?" Sloan is referring to the upcoming hospital stay and Step-Dad nods stubbornly.

"No. You stay here, live your life and live it well. I want us both to remember today, not the last few years, or me wasting away to nothing. Okay?"

Sloan nods, smiling weakly. This is closure for him and even though he's hurting – and hurting badly, I think he will be okay. We ride across town in a cab and Step-Dad drops us off in front of Sloan's apartment. While the driver hops out of the front seat to pull the bike from the trunk, the clouds part slightly from the sky and dewy sun-rays pour onto the sidewalk. Step-Dad climbs out of the car behind Sloan and gives him another big hug. Both are struggling not to cry as Step-Dad slides into the backseat once again and Sloan carefully closes the door behind him.

Sloan waits on the curb with his bike resting against his thigh as the cab pulls away and heads down the street, toward the airport.

What a day, huh?

He doesn't make it to bed until after midnight. For the first time in weeks I had to nag him to brush his teeth and take his vitamins. He placed his cell phone on the bedside table, ignoring the blinking message light. I know he's concerned about talking to Sandy and we both think it's her who has left a message, but he's not ready to call her back. Not yet.

Their first kiss was a few days ago and it turned into a full on hands-beneath-the-clothes make-out session. I willed myself to block it out but without my own hands to cover my eyes, I saw it all. Or at least what Sloan saw, which was pretty much everything. I don't think I'll ever get used to the feeling of being trapped inside someone during intimate moments. *So gross.*

I spend the night talking to Sloan about the gun. It's time for him to get rid of it. He hasn't even thought about it for some time, which is great. But I can't stop focusing on it – not until it's gone. I feel like it might be the only real threat left for him. I spend hours delving into his sub-conscious, planting seeds, laying out scenarios, removing self-doubt and fear, until I'm actually exhausted. By the time I feel the sun behind his closed eyes, I feel like I could drift away into a deep sleep myself. *Don't I wish. I could really use a nap.*

When he wakes, his first thought is of one I planted. He squirms uncomfortably under the covers until he's flat on his back, with an arm tucked under his head, beneath the pillow. I feel a smile spread across his face and wish that he was looking into the mirror so I could enjoy the display of happiness that makes his already attractive features spectacular.

Remember that time when you were fourteen and you took Mick to the park to play catch? The sun was up high and the breeze that flowed through the trees made the park seem alive. It smelled like fresh-cut grass and wildflowers. You were there for so long that your parents came looking for you, thinking something bad had happened. You saw them before Mick did, so you told him to run long and threw the ball directly at your dad. You didn't think that Mick would actually catch it, being as uncoordinated as he was, but he did. His gloved hand closed around the ball perfectly and he jumped up and down with joy. When he realized your parents were just behind him and had seen his catch, it was all he talked about for weeks. It was one of your favorite memories with him, remember? You still have that glove and ball.

Sloan rose from under the covers and went straight to the closet, bypassing his usual morning routine of spending eons draining his bladder and dragging his long fingers through his hair till his scalp tingled. He rifled around until he found the old cardboard box and pulled it out, carrying the sacred relic back to his unmade bed. He stared at it for a moment before gently lifting the top off.

He let his hands touch the insides carefully before pulling out the glove and baseball. He rolled the old ball around in his hands, feeling the slight bumps of the worn dark-red thread beneath his skin. The white of the ball was scuffed green from their many toss excursions at the park. Mick didn't actually catch the ball all that often…except for that day.

"I remember," Sloan says softly and raises the glove to his face. He deeply inhales the smell of it before turning it over to caress Mick's faded signature in black marker. "I will always remember you, Micky."

After his morning run he showers and brushes his teeth. He's made a fruit salad…one of his favorite breakfasts now, and mixed it into a cup of cottage cheese. He remembers he has a message waiting for him on his phone, so retrieves it from his bedroom and we sit down on the couch to listen to his voicemail.

"Hi Sloan, it's Sandy. Just hoping you have a wonderful day today at work! Oh, by the way, your dad came by and I sent him your way...hope that was okay. Call me later, maybe we can do dinner? Bye!"

"Crap!" Sloan mutters.

Oops. Well, you'll have to do dinner with the 'girlfriend' another time.

I can tell he is upset but I think it's rather funny. It won't hurt her to have to wait a bit before seeing him again. I listen as the next message starts.

"Hi, I'm calling for Sloan Nash. This is Gladys, Dr. Perry's nurse. I have more tests results to discuss with you. Could you please give us a call when you get this message? Thank you...here is our number again...".

Sloan deletes the message before listening to the number. I assume he has it. He doesn't seem at all irritated or concerned about the call, so I don't push it. He was already tested for every STD under the sun months ago and all the serious things were ruled out.

He's dialing on his phone and I realize he's calling Sandy. I want to yawn...I actually *feel* tired. But I also want to roll my eyes and clear my throat just to remind him that I'm here.

Blah, blah, blah, blah. I mumble to myself as he talks to Sandy briefly. When they hang up he goes back into the bedroom and gathers up Mick's glove – tucking the ball tightly inside. He wanders around the living room until he finds a place to display the glove. He decides to stash it in the middle of the small entertainment system – on a shelf. From where he placed it, you can see it clearly from the living room, dining table and small kitchen. He seems happy with it there.

I love it. I tell him.

He goes about picking up the place…washing a handful of dishes, shoving his dirty hamper deeper into the corner where it can't be easily seen. He's preparing for *her*. He even changes his sheets and remakes his bed.

As he moves about the house I start to feel a schism form between us. *What's that?* I feel suspended, like I'm floating. Suddenly that pinching sensation is back.

Oh, no! It's happening…I'm going back!

I really start to panic as it closes in around me and I try and use my mind to hold onto him, but the void is growing. I'm being pushed, or pulled out of Sloan.

I'm not done here! I shout.

What about the gun? He still has it, I haven't gotten him to get rid of it yet, surely I can't leave with the weapon still loaded and hidden in his closet? The pinching is now at my waist and I can actually feel my body again.

Wait! I'm not done…please! I shout louder, but he doesn't hear me. My vision through his eyes narrows, like I'm staring out into a long tunnel. As the pinching over my missing body becomes an intense pulling sensation, I try once more to be heard.

Sloan, please be safe! Don't forget me...don't forget me...my name is Piper...Piper Willow.

♥

I'm not sure why I do that...say my name at the last minute. It's not as if it would ever matter, him hearing my name...and besides – I don't think he was listening to me anyway. I wasn't needed anymore after-all. I feel myself surrounded by a heavy darkness and my mind pulls nearly apart before it's reunited with my body. I miss him already.

.

CHAPTER 14

The first thing I notice is the cold glass ground below my feet. I wiggle my toes and relish the feeling. After wrapping my arms around my chest and waist, I hug myself tightly. *I did it! I saved someone!* The door opens and the small room is flooded with the bright white light of the Station. I didn't think I'd miss it but I know now that I did.

I step through the doorway, anxious to tell Niles about my first case. But the hall is empty. *Where is he?* He said he'd be here when I came back. I release my arms from around my chest and let them fall to my side. I walk over to the portal wall and look up at where I slid my glass card in before leaving for my first case. I'm excited when I pull it from the wall because the black color has turned a smoky grey. The color reminds me of the clouds on an overcast day in San Francisco. My heart thumps a beat when I think of Sloan but my thoughts are interrupted when Niles enters the room, alarm on his face.

"Niles! I can't wait to tell you everything...hold on, what's wrong?"

He comes up to me and gives me a quick hug. "I'm sorry I arrived late, Piper, and I'm very anxious to hear about your first case. But something awful has happened, please, come with me."

I stare at him, confused and nervous at his less than cool demeanor. He's flustered, and his midnight-blue eyes are full of apprehension. I have *never* seen Niles like this. I let him take my hand and rush me out into the main hallway where there are so many people we bump shoulders. He pushes us through the sea of bewildered Volunteers and I feel a hand grip mine. I look down to see Kerry-Anne. Her brown eyes are full of alarm and the scared look on her face tells me whatever has happened is bad...really bad. We clasp our fingers around each other's hands and Kerry-Anne follows behind me as Niles guides us outside. There are so many people...people everywhere.

"I've never seen this place so full!" I shout to be heard above the roar of the crowd.

Niles is still moving quickly and even though I can't see it yet through the mass of people around us, I know we are moving toward the fountain...to the center of the Station square.

"Niles, what's happened?" I ask over his shoulder.

He doesn't look at me but mumbles, "Oh, Piper, its bad. Please, hurry dear...everyone has been called back for a meeting."

Called back? I feel my skin break out into a cold sweat almost immediately after hearing his words.

"Niles, what do you mean? Niles!"

He doesn't answer, just continues to tug me behind him as he pushes around shoulders, elbows and hips until I can finally see the top of the fountain before us. A sick feeling rolls around in my gut. Once we reach the fountain, I see three people standing on the wide rim, where Kerry-Anne and I used to sit together. Niles releases my hand and as he steps up to join them he is handed a metal clipboard by a thirty-something strikingly beautiful brunette with short brown hair that's curled up on the ends and big bangs. Her pale yellow vintage pajama top reminds me of a baby-doll outfit; the fabric is simple but the trim is lacey...very girly. The bottom of it rests high up on her thighs. She looks very 60's era to me. Two older men stand at her other side. One wears a flannel pajama set and the other is in full military duds. She is the only , and I notice that most eyes in the crowd seem to be focusing on her.

There are thousands of Volunteers and staff huddled tightly around the fountain but everyone stands very still and calm, so there is no surge pushing at my back. Kerry-Anne is clutching to my arm and I stand shoulder to shoulder with a man in his sixties, or maybe seventies...it's really hard to tell his age, but his hair is thin and white and his wrinkles are set deep into his face. I can see nothing else but a sea of limbs around me. *This is amazing.* I wonder where all these people came from and how the Station accommodates everyone without us noticing how many of us there truly are.

Niles searches the crowd and when his eyes settle on mine, he gives a little nod. Then his voice booms out above our heads, and instantly it's silent.

"Thank you everyone for your attention. As most of you have probably already figured out, you have been pulled from your Assignments for this meeting." He avoids looking in my direction but I sense his next comment is meant for me. "This is highly unusual practice, and for those of you that were on your first cases, we apologize for the confusion this may have caused."

I gasp. I wasn't ready to leave Sloan after-all. *I knew it.*

Niles continues, "We are confident that you have left your current Assignments in good condition. If this wasn't an emergency, we wouldn't have called you back on our own."

I'm shocked. I didn't think we *could* be called back from an assignment early. And Niles…I want to know who he is *exactly*, because now I understand he's much more than just my Intake Specialist.

A murmur has spread through part of the crowd to my right and Niles holds up his hand for their attention. His blue sweater-vest glows against the blue tile of the fountain, and for one brief moment I want to laugh…because the dark turquoise colors match perfectly. The whispering group immediately quiets.

"Edith will explain to you what has happened." He steps slightly away from the brunette woman, who smiles weakly at the crowd.

"Who is she?" Kerry-Anne whispers at my shoulder.

"I don't know. I've never seen her before," I whisper back with a gentle shake of my head and a subtle lift of my shoulder.

"Hello everyone. And thank you, Niles." She pauses to smile at him and I see a subtle look exchange between them. Something more than friendship seems to pass between their gazes. *No way. Could there be love in the after-life? Well, that's...surprising.*

"To start, I feel it is incumbent to mention this is not something that happens often here at the Station. In fact, I remember only one other case such as this in my time as one of your mentors."

Mentor. Ah...so that's what she's called. Does this mean that Niles is a 'mentor' too?

"Some of you that were removed from your current cases are New Arrivals. And to ensure that what has happened does not happen again, we have brought all of you here today to make doubly certain that all New Arrivals are *completely clear* of the Station's rules and expectations as Volunteers. Those of you that are seasoned Volunteer's and staff members are here as a reminder that even you can make mistakes."

Oh wow.

"You all know that after your orientation, training sessions and the invaluable time you have spent with your Intake Specialist, our number one job here at the Station is to help prevent others from taking their own lives. This is what we do. Those who choose not to devote the rest of their existence here can opt-out at any time."

The crowd is deathly quiet. *Oh, get on with it, what's happened?*

She takes a deep breath before continuing. "One of our New Arrival Volunteer's has helped his Assignment commit suicide." Everyone gasps this time, including me.

♥

Niles stands absolutely still, with his mouth pressed into a straight, tight line. The two men on the other side of Edith gaze out at the crowd with wary expressions. I look around me nervously, wondering if the Volunteer she mentioned is here somewhere hiding in the crowd. Apparently, I'm not the only one with this idea, since everyone seems to be taking long, hard looks at their neighbors.

Kerry-Anne grips onto my arm even tighter. "Who do you think it was?" She asks over the low but growing sounds of whispered hushes around us.

"I don't know."

I shake my head slowly from side to side, and catch a glimpse of Niles looking in my direction. I feel my body tense and chill. Is he looking at...*me*? No, he can't be. I know exactly what happened with Sloan, and he was alive and well when I was pulled back to the Station. The people that stand around me start to move away. I glance down quickly at

Kerry-Anne but she is almost a foot shorter than I am and it seems as if Niles is looking right *at* me…or maybe it's just above me?

I turn around slowly and standing just inches behind me is Beady Eyes. The impatient, chunky boy from my first training class backs away from me when our eyes lock. Even though no one has said it yet, I know without a doubt and he must see it on my fearful expression. *He is the one.*

Kerry-Anne jumps against me when Niles calls out loudly in our direction. "Joseph Selfridge, please come here."

I gape at Beady Eyes as he blanches at the mention of his name and slowly pushes past me, moving at a snail's pace toward the fountain where the four Mentors wait quietly with flat expressions. His sweat pants hang awkwardly around his thick waist and his tight undershirt hugs every pudgy inch of his torso. Many people at the Station are barefoot but Beady Eyes is wearing a pair of faded *Sketchers* that squeak softly when he walks. I move my naked feet away from his instinctually, remembering how he stepped on me with no regard, or remorse, before our first training class.

After Beady Eyes reaches the fountain, he stands with his arms at his thighs, tugging on the sides of his pants, looking down at the ground like a young child waits for a reprimand. His head hangs low while he shuffles his feet nervously.

What are they going to do to him?

Edith speaks softly but loud enough that I'm sure most of the onlookers can still hear her. "Joseph, you have intentionally violated our most cardinal rule." She glares down at his thick brown hair. He still hangs his head and hasn't looked up at her yet. I don't blame him. I'm scared, myself. Edith continues, "We have two basic functions here. One: Train those who choose to become Volunteers so that they may save a life. Two: Help those that opt-out of volunteering to move on."

The crowd stands in silence, not breathing, not moving. Kerry-Anne squeezes tighter onto my arm and I use my free hand to pat her wrist, reassuringly. I'm thankful in that moment that we can't experience pain anymore. I'm pretty sure the circulation in my arm is cut off and that she is only an ounce of pressure away from popping my arm right out of my shoulder joint.

"Look at me, Joseph." Edith says the words carefully but forcefully.

After a long pause, he tilts his head up slightly to meet Edith's icy stare. I can see that the side of his face is trembling and I'm sure he's crying. Her expression softens slightly but she is still glaring at him in a way that I hope she *never* looks at me. "Since you have broken every rule imaginable as a Volunteer and not only allowed, but *encouraged* your Assignment to kill himself, you have forfeited your right to remain here at the Station."

A low rumble picks up momentum through the crowd but quiets when Niles raises a hand above his head. Niles can be scary too, if he needed to be. His face shows no signs of his usual gentle demeanor. I don't allow us to make eye contact because I'm sure I'd cry if he ever looked at me this way.

"Have you anything to say?" She asks the words curtly and Joseph Beady Eyes shakes his head slowly.

She continues immediately, "You have no choice but to move on, Joseph."

Oh no. Does this mean he moves on...like to the next place, or does this mean he moves on to a Hell of his own making?

When my eyes dart over to Niles again, he is now looking at Joseph Beady Eyes with a sad expression. I think I understand which version of moving on Edith is referring to. And it's my turn to squeeze Kerry-Anne's arm. I bite down on my lip to keep it from trembling.

"Please go with Hector, Joseph. You need to be processed out of the Station."

The man in the military outfit steps down from the fountain rim and nods at Joseph Beady Eyes to walk with him. I wonder why he hasn't said one word in his defense. *Maybe he has none?* He walks slowly next to Hector as a wide berth is created in front of them. People clear the space quickly, almost like they are afraid of making any physical contact with the Volunteer who failed...*on purpose.*

Why would he do that? I imagine every moment I had with Sloan. Never once did I think he *should* die. I have so many questions, but I'm not sure who to ask. We all watch as Hector and Joseph Beady Eyes...forever to be known now as the Volunteer Who Killed His Assignment, walk briskly away. They enter the main door to the Admissions Department and I wonder briefly if Tight Bun Lady is waiting inside for him with paperwork in hand. This time, I don't laugh.

CHAPTER 15

I walk with Kerry-Anne to the Staff building with a large group of teen Volunteers. Some of them I've seen before but I don't know most of the young faces. Niles is somewhere up front, leading the group. We slowly file into the meeting room where I met Mallory for the first time. I end up on the far-side of the table, with Kerry-Anne still tightly wrapped around my arm. Slowly I start recognizing the others who were in Orientation with me. All except the one boy who chose to opt-out on his own.

Niles is standing at the head of the table with his hands resting on top of the oversized black office chair. He waits patiently as the tail-end of the large group struggles to fit into the room. Bodies are pressed all around me and I try to make my narrow frame as small as possible. A tall boy wearing nothing but his boxer-briefs leans against my right hip. I'm not sure whether to laugh at the close contact with a practically nude boy, or cry. *Whatever you do, don't look down.* I tell myself this as I chew on my lower lip. It's not an appropriate time to laugh *or* cry.

A loud throat-clearing commands the room and I look at Niles as he begins to speak. "Thank you everyone for your patience. My name is Niles Abbott. Some of you know me as a Station Mentor; a few of you know me as your Intake Specialist. I've been asked to pull your age group aside while the other Mentor's do the same with the rest of your fellow Volunteers. I'll try and make this quick so that you can all get back to work."

Oh good. Back to Sloan! My heart picks up an extra beat or two. *Wow, I really miss him.*

"First though, let me explain to you what has happened. After that, I'll take your questions…and then you can go back to the Consignment Department to pick up your next case."

Wait, what? Our next *case?* Nervously, I finger the cool glass card that is tucked into the waistband of my sleep shorts.

"So, I'm sure you put together by now that Mr. Selfridge, in short…*failed* as a Volunteer. We don't use that term here for many reasons. You all know that you can't force your Assignments to make the right or safe choices you suggest."

I laugh on the inside, because I know differently. I remember screaming at Sloan to get up by making him think he was on fire. The memory makes me smile a bit, but I turn my attention back to Niles.

"…Since you can't *force* your Assignments to succeed, we don't consider their deaths as your

144

failure. What happened with Mr. Selfridge is completely different. It would be a violation of his Assignment's confidentiality to discuss with you the details of his case, but what I can say, is that he was a very needy person. Mr. Selfridge gave up on assisting his needs. In fact, he encouraged the young man to take his own life and that of several other people, which is why you won't see this Assignment here at the Station."

Some of us gasp, some of us murmur. I stand still and quiet, slightly horrified and even more so - confused. I don't get why Beady Eyes would become a Volunteer if he didn't want to truly help someone. It's selfish beyond the definition of the word. I would die...many times over...to save Sloan.

"...As Miss Edith explained, this doesn't happen often. It's very rare, so rare in fact that we don't have an actual protocol in place for handling such situations. The only option was to force Mr. Selfridge to move on. And he didn't move on to the next phase of the journey that you all will eventually take, if you continue doing exceptional jobs as Volunteers."

Oh, this is new. It's been mentioned vaguely in brief conversations that there is something after the Station, though no one, even Niles, seems to understand what it is.

"Something happened with Mr. Selfridge's group of New Arrivals that frankly scared the other Mentors, including myself. All of you received your First Assignment rather quickly and your matches were...not typical." He pauses to let this sink in.

I look around the room. First at Kerry-Anne, who seems confused and not sure what Niles is saying, and then I search out each and every one of the teens that I remember from my Orientation.

Niles continues, "So, we were afraid that perhaps there wasn't enough solid training for this particular group, or that something in the matching process went awry, and we brought back every Volunteer…with the exception of a few very seasoned people who were on top priority cases."

Top priority? I didn't know there was such a thing.

"After reviewing the cases that all New Arrivals received, it seems that all of them have been extremely dedicated Volunteers. And this makes us very happy." His eyes flick to mine and he smiles briefly at me. I gulp and force myself to smile faintly back.

"Now. I know some of you were in various stages of your cases when you were brought back. Unfortunately, you cannot return to the same Assignment once you leave, we don't have the ability to send you back. Our hope is that you left an impression that will make a difference. That's all we can expect from those cases."

I'm so sad I think I might cry and I bite down on my lip again. Hard.

"What you can do now, is return to the Consignment Department and let them know you are ready for your next case. Unless you feel you need more training, which is always open for New or Old Arrivals. I think I've covered most of the basics, do you have any questions?"

I can't go back to see Sloan. So no, I don't have any questions.

♡

"Piper, can you wait for just a minute, please?"

Crap. I was hoping I could sneak outside before Niles caught me. I just need some fresh air. Though I'm not sure if outside really *is* outside, at least there aren't overcrowded meeting rooms with half-naked boys to rub hips with.

I nod at him and step back against the wall to let the other's file out into the hallway. Kerry-Anne stands hesitantly at my side, so I lean down and hug her.

"Don't worry. Meet me at the fountain?" I ask.

"Sure." She smiles and falls behind the tall semi-nude guy that was standing near us. She's one of the last to exit the room. Suddenly I feel anxious to be alone with Niles, as if I'm in trouble. I really don't want him to be angry with me.

Did I do something wrong with Sloan?

"Please, sit down Piper." He smiles gently and I let some of the anxiety fade away.

After we settle into chairs, Niles leans forward and pats my leg. "I am so sorry your first case ended the way it did. But I'd love to talk to you about it. If you are still willing?"

"Oh! Sure." This isn't where I was expecting the conversation to go and I relax into the chair a bit more.

"Piper, are you okay?" Niles scrunches his forehead into a wrinkled V pattern which makes me smile.

"I'm okay. I'm just worried about Sloan." I look down at my hands.

"Ah, yes, Sloan. You liked him very much, didn't you?" He smiles again and there is a hint of something playful in his look. I think he's teasing me!

Rather than give him the benefit of the doubt, I simply nod my head up and down a few times. He reaches up to rub his chin before leaning back into his chair, stretching his legs out under the massive glass table.

"Sloan is an interesting case. It's true that he's a very wounded boy but he has so much potential. He's not bad looking either, is he?" He laughs when I gawk at him.

"How do you know about him?" I ask.

"Well, all Intake Specialists know about the cases their Volunteers are on. Though I have to say, Sloan was an interesting match for you. I would have expected your first to be with another girl, about your age. That's how it works, usually." He pauses with a curious look on his face.

"Yeah, I was really surprised that my first case had a penis too."

Niles laughing is a wonderful sound to hear after the events earlier.

"Yes, that must have been a shock." He chuckles a bit more before leaning forward and propping his elbows on his knees.

"From what I was able to see, Piper, I think you did a great job with him."

My heart swells at his approval. "Thanks. I wasn't sure sometimes if I was doing it right." I admit.

"Doing it right? Whatever do you mean?" He raises an eyebrow at me.

"You know, my job," I answer him. "It was harder sometimes than I thought it would be."

He nods as if he's considering what I said carefully. He reaches out to take my hand in his before speaking. "Piper dear, you will be an exceptional Volunteer and I've known this since you first arrived. Please don't doubt yourself. That won't help you here, or your cases down the road. Do you understand what I'm saying?"

"I think so. You want me to believe in myself," I say as I blink back tears. A loose strand of my ash-blonde hair hangs over my eye. I push it behind my ear and take a deep breath, inhaling the subtle aroma of grapefruit.

"Yes, dear. Because if you can't believe in yourself after all you've been through, you are of no help to your future Assignments. Just like Joseph." He says his name sadly and for a second I almost forget who he is talking about.

"What's going to happen to him?" I ask softly.

"Oh, he's already gone, dear. Somewhere where he will be lost in pain and alone with his inner demons forever. It's heartbreaking but it was the only other option for him." I can tell that he's genuinely affected by what has happened.

"Why did he do it?" I ask Niles.

He shakes his head slowly. "No one knows why, Piper. But it's just so sad that his Assignment not only took his life but also several of his fellow school-mates. It's just an awful thing all around."

Several school-mates? No! Oh, Beady Eyes...how could you let this happen?

"How old were they?" My voice is squeaky, like an injured mouse.

"The oldest victim was seventeen and the youngest was two days away from his fifteenth birthday." Niles rubs at his chin then ends the conversation with a terse nod. "We shouldn't be talking about this. It's not our concern, plus, we have other things to discuss before you take your next Assignment."

Something occurs to me then, a question I didn't want to ask in front of a group of strangers. "Niles, why are you a Mentor and my Intake Specialist as well?"

"I'm actually phasing out of my job as an Intake Specialist. Soon I won't be taking any more New Arrivals."

I feel myself blanch with panic. If he's no longer my Intake Specialist, who will take care of me? Could I be assigned to someone awful like Tight Bun Lady?

"No need to worry, dear. My Volunteers will always remain my responsibility, so I will always be your Intake Specialist." He stands and pulls me up to my feet.

"Niles? You mentioned some Volunteers have special Assignments. Why?" I ask as he slowly moves me toward the door.

"Our seasoned Volunteers have been through almost any scenario you can imagine. It is those special people that we choose for cases that take special care. Our children, people of major importance in the world, that have the ability to do real damage on a grand scale...people like that. Those of the opposite sex are usually assigned seasoned Volunteers as well, which is why it was a little surprising that you were given Sloan as your first case." He stops to look down at me before taking a deep breath.

I think he's tired, tired of his job. I don't know how long he's been here. But right now doesn't seem like the appropriate time to ask about it.

"So, there is one thing I wanted to ask you..." he smiles and laughs a little, "...what gave you the idea to use yourself as a fire alarm to wake your Assignment? Because that, my dear, was *brilliant*."

Trish Marie Dawson

CHAPTER 16

Niles listens to me with great interest as I recap the last two months with Sloan. Sometimes he laughs, sometimes he seems solemn and lost in thought, but when I'm done he appears to be very pleased with the outcome of my first case. I'm looking for Kerry-Anne's yellow sundress as we slowly approach the fountain, having just left the Ones Building. There were fewer children inside playing than before but it's still nice to watch them. I really wish I knew where they moved on to. The sounds of their laughs are infectious and I love that Niles brings me there when we talk.

"There's your friend, are you meeting her?" Niles gestures to our right where Kerry-Anne sits alone, twirling the hem of her sundress in between her fingers.

"We were going to talk before heading back to the Consignment Building. I wish we could take longer breaks before being assigned a new case."

I stick my lower lip out in a pout and I am so thankful I have my face to make these expressions. The worst part of being a Volunteer is being trapped in someone else's mind without your own body. It's impossible for me to express my emotions with just my mind.

"You can go to Training." Nile says with a smile.

"Right, cause that's a break." We both laugh.

"Piper!"

I hear Kerry-Anne's shy voice an octave higher than usual and glance over my shoulder to wave at her. She seems excited, no doubt ready to share details about our Assignments. We aren't allowed to share names or specifics – that would be a confidentiality violation.

I hug Niles goodbye and watch him walk into the Admissions Department. When I get close enough for physical contact, Kerry-Anne launches herself at me and wraps her thin arms around my back, squeezing me to her. This sort of physical contact is unusual from her. It makes me curious to find out what has her in such a good mood as I usher her toward the fountain rim to sit.

"Spill!"

It's all I have to say to give her permission to speak first. She is beaming while she talks. Her brown eyes are aglow with life and I watch with fascination as her glossy black hair brushes her shoulders as if it's alive when she moves her head up, down and side to side.

My dirty-blonde hair has always been a little too dry and completely unreasonable in any sort of weather. The slightest rise in humidity would make the baby curls around my hairline pop up, causing a rather unsightly curly-halo effect around my face. Beach days were the worst. My hair would end up tangled and looking stringy everywhere but around my temples and forehead, where every short hair would be standing at frizzy attention by the end of the day. But the streak-blonde color I got by the end of summer made all the bad-hair days completely worth it.

I doubted Kerry-Anne *ever* had bad hair days. I try imagining her with frizzed out curls around her face and it makes me giggle softly. I stifle it before she hears me by coughing into my hand. There's no need for coughing at the Station since no one can get sick, but it works...she continues on with her story about her first Assignment. She was fifteen, two months younger than Kerry-Anne and from what it sounds like...they were a perfect match.

"She was just great! I'm so happy she's better now, you know? But my second Assignment, oh my gosh, she was a handful. She-" I raise my hand in surprise and Kerry-Anne stops talking mid-sentence.

"Wait, your *second* Assignment? How many have you been on?"

"I've only been on two. It goes by so slow in the real world, not like the time here. How many have you had?" She asks.

"I was pulled back during my first." I glower.

I'm still upset that I was ripped away from Sloan before he was ready...before *I* was ready. Kerry-Anne reaches her hand out and pats my knee affectionately. I've started to see her as the little sister I never had, except of course minus all the drama of actually having a younger sibling.

"I'm so sorry. First Assignments are very special." She looks down at her sandaled feet.

"It's okay. Actually, I think he's going to be fine."

I hope that's true.

"*He?*"

Kerry-Anne balks at me. Her thin, red lips form a perfect circle as she stares at me with her mouth wide open, her large and round eyes unblinking.

"Oh yeah, he was a *he* all right. And sort of gorgeous." I laugh because Kerry-Anne looks mortified.

"Was there a problem with your match?" She almost whispers the question, as if she is afraid of someone hearing us. The only people around are a few passerby's moving in between buildings. For this rare moment in time, we have the fountain to ourselves.

"Actually Niles told me that it happens but he said it's rare for your first case. I guess the older Volunteers typically get matched with the opposite sex more often."

"What does that mean then, that you were matched to a guy?" She asks nervously.

I shrug. "Who knows, maybe I'm special." I wink at her, which lightens her mood back to what it was before and we begin comparing notes about our cases again. And of course I know what Kerry Anne's first question about Sloan will be just before she asks it.

"What were the showers like?"

I hang around the fountain for what seems like decades, waiting for the crowds to clear out of the Station. I imagine some if not most of the Volunteers will go back on assignment right away. But the Consignment building is packed and there is such a constant state of motion through the front door that I decide to just sit back and wait a little while longer. Kerry-Anne hung out with me at first until Mallory showed up. I could tell Kerry-Anne was anxious for her next case, so I hugged her and wished her well before she headed off toward the Station's busiest building to wait in line with the others for her next case.

"How are you?" Mallory asks me.

"I'm okay, still a bit upset I guess about being brought back early."

"Yeah, me too," she says.

I stretch out along the rim of the fountain so I'm on my stomach and I love the feeling of the cool tile on my bare legs and arms. After dipping my fingers into the fountain and swirling the crystal clear water around into a mini-whirlpool, Mallory rolls onto her stomach and gently plunges her hand into the water next to mine. Her head is just inches away and I can smell grapefruit again.

"Mallory?" I ask.

"Hmm?"

"Why does our hair smell like grapefruit?"

Mallory pushes up onto her elbows and then her upper body shakes with laughter. When she's done she wipes a few tears from her eyes before she answers. "Oh wow, I haven't laughed like that in too long. I really don't know, but I can't tell you how many times I've wondered the same thing."

She grins at me and I resume my hand twirling in the cold water. She's still giggling when she lies back down.

"You two look quite comfortable. Almost as if you're on vacation, or something."

We both look up to see Carlson Smith standing over us. For a moment I don't remember him, but then I see the metal clipboard in his hand and I vaguely recall meeting him just after my arrival. He called Niles 'Abbott'. I'm surprised again by how thin he is. Each bone in his body is visible beneath his worn shirt but his eyes are full of life. He looks briefly at me before his gaze settles on Mallory and he begins to fidget with the pocket of his flannel pajama pants. He seems nervous around her and no wonder…Mallory is a very beautiful girl. All curves, legs and blonde hair. I imagine it's impossible for her to go unnoticed by any of the men at the Station.

She smiles weakly at Carlson before pushing up onto her knees, taking care to tuck her skirt around her legs discreetly. Once she's upright, his trance breaks and he looks back at me once more. I notice with a slight pang of jealousy that he doesn't look at me the way he looks at Mallory. In fact, no one at the Station does.

Figures. I'm undesirable in the after-life too. Oh, well.

Carlson clears his throat, "Piper, Niles is looking for you. I'm on my way to the gate...another New Arrival, so I told him I'd let you know," he pauses to look at Mallory once again as if he's afraid he's been caught in a lie. "If I saw you, of course."

Of course.

"Thanks," I mumble.

We watch Carlson scurry off to the gate and Mallory sighs deeply as he passes through the rusted metal in a rush and disappears into the white nothingness beyond it.

"I always feel bad when someone else arrives." She says.

"Yeah, me too."

"This time will be different, I promise. You'll be there till the end and you'll feel better when you get back."

"Good luck." I say softly.

Mallory leans in to hug me before she walks down the hall with a new ink-colored glass Assignment Card. I watch as she picks the door that leads into the Depot room and turn to see Niles grinning at me.

"What?"

"It's wonderful to see the two of you getting on this well. I was a bit worried, dear, after that initial meeting." He smiles. Gentle, as always.

"She's a nice girl. I can see why she was chosen as my Volunteer. But don't get too excited, we aren't BFF's just yet." I reply with a wink.

"BFF's? What is that?"

It's my turn to giggle. "Best Friends Forever."

"Ah, the young...always so eager to shorten the English language."

"Yep."

I smile at him as I search for my name on the giant volunteer billboard. Nothing yet. I finger the glass disk that is hanging around my neck, remembering the first time it went off, how I thought my chest was on fire. The memory seems so long ago, but it's impossible to tell time in the Station; there are no days, no nights and no clocks. I can't tell if I've been here for five minutes or five years.

If I had died with a watch on, would it work here?

"Piper." Niles distracts me from my mental wandering. "They're ready for you."

I look down to see the glass light up inside my palm.

It's time again.

CHAPTER 17

I try to remain calm this time as the pinching starts at my feet and slowly works its way up my body but it feels too much like crawling ants that I attempt to rub the sensation off my skin anyway. Niles told me that this part of the transition feels a little different for each Volunteer. Some have described it as a tickle, others as hot pokers being jammed into their skin. I guess I'm somewhere in between and should feel relieved but I can't *not* imagine thousands of tiny bugs scampering up my body and pinching me. The thought sends me near the edge of panic once again.

Just when I'm ready to scream, it stops. I am expecting darkness, like when I first arrived on Sloan's case. But my new Assignment isn't asleep; she's awake and walking somewhere. The light that floods in around me is at first disorienting and I struggle to focus on the images that pass by us in a flash. A door with a window that takes up the top half flies by on our right. A row of metal lockers fly by on our left. And there are people...kids - everywhere. We are in some sort of hallway. Doors, lockers, teenagers. *Great. This is a school.*

Unlike Sloan, this Assignment does not guard her emotions (and I know it's a girl, because her mental female imprint is so strong and *nothing* like Sloan) and they flood through me in a frenzied, unbalanced way that at first I can't process one single thought. It's like picking through a pile of hay for a needle...except in *this* mind, the pile of hay is more like the size of a football field and I'm looking for one particular blade of grass.

I imagine I'm in a car and that I am slamming my foot down on the brake.

Stop! I scream loudly.

And she does, long enough to lean against a wall and pick at the edge of her math textbook. She looks around the hallway hesitantly and I'm overwhelmed with a feeling I haven't experienced so fiercely since Bree went flying through my windshield. *Fear. She's afraid.* So much so that her body is trembling and her mind is scattered like dried up maple leaves on a windy autumn day being blown along an empty street.

Okay. Let's calm down. I speak to her gently, knowing if I yell again, I might very well send her fragile mental state running to the hills.

Take a deep breath, inhale...exhale.

She immediately complies, surprisingly, and I feel oxygen rush through her body, lowering her heart rate just a tad. Based on the height of the others that pass by us, I'm assuming she's small.

The kids are definitely high school aged and not one stops to smile or say hi.

I pick through her mind trying to find the source of her fear, but instead of locating it in the tangled, manic mess of her memories, it's suddenly staring us in the face. I feel my Assignment shrink against the wall like a trapped rabbit as her heart-rate skyrockets. A click of wannabe Kardashian sisters has strolled up to us, intentionally surrounding my poor Assignment, trapping her against the cold plaster wall. I know this is the source of her fear and I hate these girls *instantly*.

"Hey, Goggles," the tallest girl says. "When'd you get the new hardware?" She reaches toward my Assignment and pushes her glasses up the bridge of her nose, painfully smashing them into her face.

What the hell!

"Um." My Assignment is pressing herself hard into the wall, with nowhere to run.

"Ivy, let's go," says one of the girls with a flip of her long, dark hair over her shoulder, "Mr. Fyne is coming." Her large, brown eyes remind me of a giant sink-hole.

"In a minute," the first brunette with legs that seem to start just below the neck snaps as she glances briefly down the hall. "Where's your new boyfriend at?" She turns her attention back to my Assignment.

"Huh?" I feel my Assignment's panic rising around me.

Calm down. It will be okay. I try to comfort her.

A little too sweetly, Ivy repeats her question. "Where's your *boyfriend* at?"

When my Assignment doesn't answer, Ivy leans forward and hisses into her ear. "He's only hanging out with you because he feels sorry for your ass."

"Ivy." The empty-eyed girl hisses nervously.

"Shut up Lauren. I *know*."

Lauren's bottomless eyes dart back down the hallway, out of my Assignment's view. I really wish she would look so I could see how close this Mr. Fyne is but she keeps her gaze firmly on the leggy Ivy. If her face wasn't full of pure evil, she'd be a beautiful girl. Her round eyes shine the color of dark coffee and even though her lips are pressed into a tight line, they are perfectly shaped and thickly coated with a light pink lip gloss that matches the blush she has colored her high cheekbones with.

Say something...anything. You have to defend yourself.

"He's not my...*boyfriend*." My Assignment speaks so quietly that only two of the three dark haired girls actually hear her.

"What?" Ivy stares at her like a wolf cornering a lamb.

You can do this. Defend yourself.

Even though I have no idea which boy they are referring to, I know that if my Assignment doesn't defend herself against girls like this, the torture will be relentless.

Ivy glowers at us. Just as she opens her mouth to talk, a male voice speaks harshly over my Assignment's left shoulder and the three girls quickly step back.

"What's going on girls?" The man is still out of my view...but by the sound of his voice I know he's close, very close.

"Nothing, Mr. Fyne, we were just checking to see if Abby here got her notes from yesterday's English class." Ivy smiles innocently over my Assignment's shoulder. *Ohhh, I want to smack her a good one.*

"Right. Well, let's move along to your next class, okay?"

The girls nod at Mr. Fyne and all three toss their long, brown hair over their shoulders in unison as they walk away, quickly becoming lost in the full hallway of high-schooler's. My Assignment watches as they disappear before turning to face her savior.

Mr. Fyne is *fine*. A tall, dark-haired Greek God stands before us. I haven't looked at a man quite like I am looking at this one. His clothes are stretched out to accommodate every inch of his chiseled body. My lower jaw has detached itself from my head back at the Station and hit the floor with a solid 'clunk'. *This man is way too good-looking to be a teacher!* I guess it's good to know that even after everything I've been through, I can still find an attractive man...well, *attractive*.

"Everything okay, Abiline?" His ruby lips break apart slightly as he smiles and everywhere angels break out into chorus.

"Yeah." Abby, or *Abiline* says. "Just on my way to History."

I notice that she seems completely immune to Mr. Fyne's gorgeousness. I can't imagine a sixteen year old being able to form a full sentence around him. I know I couldn't. I'm surprised and a bit intrigued by her lack of interest. Not that it's a bad thing, he's her *teacher*…and she's still very much a kid. But I'm not. So I stare when given the chance.

"I'll walk with you." He smiles, and there go the angels again.

She shrugs but manages a small smile in return, and Mr. Fyne walks just beside her down the hall. Of course, every other girl stops to bat her eyes or say hi to him. He's polite to them all but not overly so. I imagine he's one of the most popular teachers in the school. I wonder what his subject is. I hope that Abby doesn't actually have him for one of her classes, he's simply too distracting. My job does not include drooling over teachers.

"Well, this is it, right?" We've stopped in front of one of the classrooms and Abby nods shyly.

"Thanks," she says.

His bright blue eyes shine down at her when he smiles and I find myself getting lost in them. His pupil is encircled by a dark green color, making the blue almost glow. My skin is flushing with those stupid raging hormones again…somewhere. I immediately feel guilty and mentally slap myself across the face. *Focus, Piper. Keep your focus.*

"Any time, Abiline."

She turns to walk through the door when Mr. Fyne puts a hand on her arm, gently. "Abiline, ignore those girls, okay? They aren't worth your time." His beautifully sculpted face sets into a serious expression.

"Sure," Abby says, her voice thick with emotion.

Oh no, don't cry. Not at school, or they'll never let you forget it…you can do this. Whatever *this* is.

We leave Mr. Fyne standing outside in the hall with a concerned look on his face. When we walk into the room, Abby hurries to a desk in the back and is followed by the stares of everyone in the class. Something big has obviously happened. I know that she is in danger, which is why I'm here of course. But I won't be able to get a handle on her emotions until she's in a much calmer, quieter place. Right now my biggest concern is getting *both* of us through this school day without swooning over the school staff or decking a fellow student.

Trish Marie Dawson

CHAPTER 18

I finally get a good look at Abby when she hides in the bathroom during lunch time. I already knew she wore glasses so that wasn't a surprise and I was certain she was small but I'm still taken aback slightly by exactly *how* tiny she is. She's less than five feet for sure, with a thick head of dull-brown frizzy hair.

Honey, you are in desperate need of a good conditioner and a flat-iron. We'll work on that later.

Even behind her glasses, her eyes are lovely. The amber color of her irises reminds me of hot coals from a fire. The features of her face, like her body, are all small. Thin, heart-shaped lips, button-like nose, small and pointy chin, and narrow eyebrows that she'll be happy to not have to pluck when she gets older. She's cute, almost elf-like. But I can see why she is teased at school. She's different. I like her.

Are you going to eat your lunch in here?

In silent answer, she walks away from the bathroom mirror to the last toilet stall and goes inside, closing and latching the door behind her. She sets her back-pack between her feet and pulls out a small brown bag with a smashed PB&J sandwich and a bruised apple inside. Poor kid, it seems she doesn't have a home-maker parent to send her off with awesome bagged lunches. I remember all the times I wished my own mother was around to send me to school with packed meals and I want to cry for Abby. Despite who she lives with, I can tell she is alone. I remember this feeling all too well.

She nibbles at the sandwich and takes two bites of the apple before carefully wrapping the food up in a napkin and placing it back in the wrinkled bag. She's still working on swallowing her food when the bathroom door opens, banging into the wall. Several girls enter, laughing and talking loudly. Abby sits motionless on the toilet rim, with partially chewed food tucked into one of her cheeks. She tilts her head to the side and listens nervously to the clamoring group of girls that must be fawning over themselves at the mirrors. I hear at least four different voices, all begin to talk over each other.

"I heard that the whole family is full of crazies."

"Yeah, and did you know that he lost it a few years ago and tried to kill her and her mom?"

"Are you serious?!"

"Well, it explains why she's so weird, you know?"

"I would leave too, if I was her mom."

"Why's she even here still? The school should totally kick her out. I mean, isn't she like dangerous or something?"

"For sure. I don't trust her. I bet she walks around with one of her daddy's guns in that ugly bag of hers."

They all laugh. Abby sits so still that I'm not sure if she's listening aptly, or in a state of shock. When the stall door next to us opens with a bang, Abby jumps and pulls her backpack up her legs where she cradles it to her chest. She's struggling to not cry.

Sshh. It's okay. It's okay.

After a brief conversation about the cute boys on the football team, the girls eventually leave the bathroom and Abby finally lets out a few quiet sobs. I really wish I could hug her. The poor girl needs some comforting. But all I have are words; words that she may or may not be able to hear.

After school today, let's go to your favorite quiet place, okay?

I *really* need to figure out what's going on. I keep getting flash memories that don't make sense. Her head is too jumbled up for me to wade through it while she's in this environment. I do know one thing though: she's much closer to the end then Sloan *ever* was.

After the final bell rings Abby practically runs down the street to get away from the school grounds. She hasn't talked to anyone besides teachers all day. She has no friends, in fact, it's almost like the entire school hates her. She's so sweet, I don't understand it.

She walks briskly down the streets for almost half an hour until we reach a heavily wooded area. Abby flanks the over-grown trees until we reach a railroad crossing. Weeds and grasses have grown over the edges of the rail but I'm still concerned for her safety as Abby begins to walk along it, following the slight curve of the tracks into the woods.

When I said to go somewhere quiet, I didn't mean for you to pick a completely deserted place where who knows what sort of creeps linger! And get off the tracks, are you crazy?

Abby ignores me and continues south until a small gap in the trees opens up to her right. She leaves the railway and walks slowly along the unleveled green grass until she comes to a large tree with low-hanging branches. She scrambles up until she's a good twenty feet above the ground. I wish I could feel the scrape of the bark on my skin. I spent most of my childhood in trees and didn't realize until this moment that I would never be able to climb one again. I can't chastise her for scrambling up so high; it's something I would do too and I feel at home with her in the canopy.

As she looks out at the view of the woods around her, I wonder where we are. I don't recognize the scenery at all and the accents of the people in these parts are different from the West Coast. I wait for her mind to start settling, but it's still racing wildly with thoughts of school, family and...*death*?

Eventually I'm able to grab onto something long enough to place us. Erie, Pennsylvania. *Wow. That's a long way from home.* Then again, *everywhere* is far from home, since home for me is now a place always aglow in blinding white light and half-naked people with bare feet that never get dirty and everyone's hair smells like yummy grapefruit.

She is staring at a tree scuff-mark on the knee of her jeans when I pull myself away from thoughts of the Station and back to her reality. Suddenly, and before I fully understand what is happening, she crawls further out on the narrow branch she was sitting on and begins to stand.

What are you doing?

Slowly she pushes up into a crouched position and hovers over the branch as it sways beneath her weight. Oh no, she's going to jump!

Don't you dare!! Sit back down, now! This is NOT what you want to do!

A small animal-like cry escapes from her mouth and she plops down onto her butt. For a second I'm afraid the sudden shift in weight is going to snap the thin branch and send Abby plummeting to the ground tangled in a mess of branches and green leaves.

Crap! You almost gave me a heart-attack!

I try not to laugh at the irony of what I've said, since I'm already dead and all but Abby has begun to cry wildly now and she is still sitting on the branch, with her size six sneakers dangling above twenty feet of open space.

It's okay Abby. Let's get off this branch, get comfortable and just take a break, okay?

She sniffles and wipes the snot from her draining nose before swiping her hand along her jeans. *Gross, but necessary, I guess.* Napkins aren't handy at the moment. After she climbs back to the tree trunk, she settles herself into the meeting place of two branches and props her legs out in front of her. From this position she isn't in danger of falling, so I relax tremendously.

"Oh, daddy," she whispers. And there it is, the flood-gates of her memory open up wide enough for a semi to drive through and I'm left digesting the fact that Abby is the daughter of a murderer.

Just over a month ago, Abby's alcoholic and sometimes drug-impaired father walked into a local liquor store and held the place up at gunpoint during a manic episode. Three hours later he was led out in handcuffs with a broken nose and a police bullet lodged in his left shoulder. He left the teller and three innocent patrons dead inside. His weapon of choice was a Colt .44 special and he fired off each bullet at whatever moved just as the police rushed the front entrance.

Abby's already fragile mother couldn't handle the angry onslaught of attention from the locals and skipped town, leaving her only child with her aging and physically disabled mother, who for the most part ignored Abby entirely.

The kids at school were the hardest part for Abby to accept. She lost the few friends she had and endured a daily assault of verbal berating and physical tormenting. Ivy, the tall and pretty brunette snake, had snatched Abby's glasses off her face in P.E. and crushed them beneath her feet just two weeks before. For whatever reason, that particular trio of girls were making it their mission to inflict all sorts of miserableness onto Abby every chance they got.

There was one boy, a former boyfriend of Ivy that stayed friendly with Abby. They weren't quite friends but at least he didn't torment her like her classmates did. Abby seemed to have warm feelings for him but I wondered if he was continuing to smile and greet Abby in the hallways just to spite his ex-girlfriend. Since he was out of town with his parents for a funeral, I couldn't form my own opinions about him just yet. For now, memories were all I had to work with. At least I found nothing of him hurting Abby as everyone else had, so he couldn't be as bad as the rest of them.

Enter in Mr. Fyne. He recently caught Ivy and one of the other girls, Shandra, cornering Abby in front of the girls' bathroom and since then he's seemed to make it his mission to wander the halls in between classes, keeping an eye on Abby. It wasn't just the students that turned on the poor girl, even some of the staff stared at her like she was harboring a communicable disease, or worse - flat-out ignored her. Not Mr. Fyne though, he seemed to truly care for Abby.

My hero.

I've waded through enough of Abby's memories to understand why she almost threw herself off the top of a tree. The next few days would be critical, so I crack my imaginary knuckles and stretch my imaginary neck, and roll my imaginary sleeves up to prepare myself for this tough case. Abby is going to need all of the training I've had and probably more, to successfully pull her back from the edge she seems ready to launch herself from.

It's not going to happen on MY shift, kiddo. We'll find a way out of the dark, don't you worry. I have big hopes for you...but for now...baby steps. When's the last time you've had a candy bar?

For girls, chocolate fixes almost everything.

After a hefty dose of dark chocolate perfection, I guide Abby home, where she can prepare for the next few days. Fortunately, her mother left many of her things behind in boxes that fill up Abby's grandmother's garage. In one of the crumpled cardboard boxes she finds what I've asked her to look for and carries the items into her room, setting them uncertainly on her bed.

She takes a shower, washes her hair and lather's it in conditioner, leaving it on for a full ten minutes before I allow her to rinse it. I have a feeling that making Abby feel better from the inside-out will help with her confidence at school. I don't want her to cross over from the innocent girl-next-door to a vain-wannabe-beauty-queen but she has absolutely no idea what to do with what she has. That's what big sisters and moms are for. Abby has neither. But she does have me. And I learned from the best…Bree.

When she's holding the flat-iron in her hand out in front of her like it's a vicious viper ready to strike, I try hard not to laugh.

Let's just see what this does for your hair, remember…baby steps. If you don't like it, you can wash your hair again and let it air-dry into its lovely frizz-filled fluffiness, I promise.

The next day we arrive at school five minutes after the last bell, on purpose. Abby rushes across the front lawn and into the double doors as if she's naked outside. I can tell by the nervous ball her stomach has become that she feels just as exposed standing in the hallway, but she's here, she's already done it…it's time to show herself off to the school.

When she opens the door to English class, I remind her to roll her shoulders back, stand up straight and smile. There's an audible gasp of surprise as she walks calmly across the room to her seat. Even the teacher has stopped mid-sentence to stare at her.

Abby sits down and carefully crosses her ankles, being sure to gently tuck her skirt in between her knees. Her hair is smooth and straight and cascades over her narrow shoulders like a chocolate fondue fountain, coming to rest at the middle of her back. I know how beautiful she looks because she spent nearly half an hour this morning staring at her reflection in the bathroom mirror.

Through the course of the day, a handful of girls have smiled at Abby and four...FOUR boys have stopped to say hi. At least ten times that many have gawked at her as she walks the halls. Even Mr. Fyne, who is her P.E. teacher, no surprise there or course, seems shocked at the change of attention she has created around her. To think some good conditioner, an hour with a flat-iron and a mega-watt smile could inflate her confidence to such heights is just amazing! She has done exactly what I wanted her to do; she's given them something *else* to talk about.

CHAPTER 19

I spend a solid week burrowing deep into Abby's mind. At night, when she is sleeping I do what I did with Sloan; prod and organize and plant little seeds of hope. Her confidence meter has gone from zero to somewhere in the millions since my arrival. She's had her school lunch with two freshmen for the last three days and they seem to genuinely not care about Abby's family drama. I hope they become good friends. With time, they just might. I know part of her success is the fact that she listens to me. It's like we have a direct line of communication, yet she is unaware that someone else is indeed talking to her. It's such a difference from Sloan, it's refreshing and thrilling to have such an eager Assignment.

It's Friday, the last day of a very long week and I've been sitting on my imaginary throne since Tuesday. Mr. Fyne no longer follows Abby's tiny shadow down the halls but he is still very friendly with her and keeps an eye on the Kardashian wannabe's during P.E. class. The trio has done little more than send scathing looks in Abby's direction but with my constant assurance that looks won't really hurt her, she has learned to ignore them for the most part. Her confidence shows.

She is crossing the wide lawn in front of the school on her way to start the day when a shrill whistle startles her. She looks to her side to see a happy-faced boy jogging in her direction. *Oh, this is the leggy chic's ex.* She stops and waves at him.

"Abiline Peterson, is that really you?" He comes to an awkward halt just a foot in front of her and leans forward, arms open wide for a hug. Abby seems surprised but lets him hug her into his broad chest. Heat radiates between them. He has light brown hair that is cut short and combed forward. He's a pretty good-looking guy, for a school jock. For a moment I think of the school jock back at home that stole the most valuable thing I had. I still hated him. Immensely. I shake my head back at the Station to clear my mind. *Come back to the present, Piper.*

"Hi, Donny. You're back." She smiles and I feel a subtle stirring of hormone's warm her insides.

Ah, I get it. Abiline and Donovan, kissing in a tree...k-i-s-s-i-n-g.

I only tease her because it makes her feel good to imagine him that way. I can tell by the scattering of her thoughts as she struggles to remain calm around Donny. He walks her inside and chats in detail about his trip out of town. When we pass Ivy and her minions in the hall, he barely nods at them. He's completely engrossed in Abby for the moment.

This is good, Abby. Very good. You are making friends and people are seeing that you are your own individual and that you shine through the darkest of times. Keep it up girly!

We part with Donny at his classroom door and Abby all but skips along to English class. She's elated. I'm elated. Until we see who is waiting for her inside the classroom talking to her teacher.

"Mom?"

♥

"Hi, Abby." Her mother stands up taller and squares her shoulders, despite the looks from students that are slowly filling the classroom.

What is she doing here?! My imaginary throne suddenly poofs into oblivion.

"Abiline, your mother has a day pass for you. Did you bring your essay?" The teacher speaks quietly, as if trying not to attract any more attention from the staring teenagers but his hushed voice does exactly the opposite.

"Um, yeah." Abby reaches into her backpack to pull out her binder. After fumbling through papers for a minute, she removes one and hands it to her teacher.

"Thanks, Abiline. Have a good day, we'll see you tomorrow." He smiles weakly before turning his attention to the whispering class.

Tomorrow? I doubt we'll be spending the whole day with dear, old mom. You'll probably see us again in ten minutes.

Abby silently follows her mother back into the now empty hallway and through the building. By the time they reach outside the temperature has dropped a bit and Abby pulls her sweater tightly around her. The autumn air has been cooling steadily in the last few days.

Ask her what she wants, Abby.

When they reach a set of benches underneath a sprawling Red Maple tree, Abby plops down onto the concrete and watches with curiosity as her mother wipes the bench clean before sitting down on the very edge. I think she's either ready to bolt or afraid of a little dirt. *Maybe both?* Somewhere I know my eyes are rolling.

"What's up, Mom?" Abby asks softly.

"I miss you. It's okay for me to miss you, isn't it?" Abby's mother tucks a loose strand of hair back into her clip.

Abby looks up and stares hard at her. "Guess you wouldn't miss me so much if you didn't take off."

The harsh edge of her words makes her mother flinch. She shuffles nervously on the bench and looks everywhere but at Abby.

"I should have taken you with me but I didn't have a place yet. I told you that. A hotel is no place for a sixteen year old girl to be living at." She looks back at Abby and her eyes are full of tears.

Abby waits a minute before speaking. "Have you heard from dad?"

"No. But I heard from his lawyer."

"Dad's got a lawyer?" Abby seems surprised and I know that no one in their family has the means or the desire to help with her father's defense.

"He has a Public Defender. It's not looking good, Abby." She pauses to look around them, probably making sure they are truly alone before continuing, "That's why I'm here. I wanted to prepare you. People might start talking."

"People are already talking, Mom." Abby's voice wavers.

And I thought she might have come to take Abby away with her.

"Baby, I know it." She says gently.

For the first time, her mother reaches out and touches her. Abby stares down at the older hand patting hers in wonder. Even before her dad's arrest, the family wasn't physically affectionate. Abby wants to pull her hand away but seems to sense that this is what her mother needs and all she can really give her, so she allows the unsolicited affection.

"So, are you staying here, or leaving?" Abby asks.

"I wasn't planning on staying, just to pick up a few things."

Oh no, she is planning on taking Abby.

"I don't want to leave Erie, Mom." I'm surprised as much as her mother is by the admission.

"Baby, no one here is going to be very kind to you over the next few months. Plus, I think I found a place for the both of us." She straightens and slowly pulls her hand away from Abby's.

"That's great and all, but I don't want to leave."

"Well, it's a good thing then that you can't come with me today. But eventually, we are both leaving this town behind us." Her mother has a faraway look in her eyes as she stares at the quiet street in front of the school.

"So you came for your things, then?" Abby tries to change the subject after an awkward minute of silence.

"Yes, just a few things I left in mama's garage." Her mother replies, but is still staring blankly out at the street.

"Can I keep your hair straightener?" Abby asks suddenly.

Her mother laughs. "Is that how you got your hair like this? It looks lovely by the way."

The two smile at each other and I almost implode with relief. Perhaps the unexpected arrival of Abby's mother will end up being a good thing. I cross my invisible fingers in hope.

♡

The two spend the day together after-all. Not that digging through poorly packed boxes in the garage is exactly quality time, but at least Abby's mother makes a genuine effort to learn about the last few weeks of her daughter's life. She seems mostly interested in anything that has to do with Donny, but Abby keeps most of her feelings quiet. I think her mother suspects Donny might mean something more to her but she doesn't push too hard for details.

"So you want to keep the straightener?" Abby's mother asks as she stands in the doorway with her arms full of bags of clothing and a small box of bathroom necessities.

"Can I?"

Abby chews nervously on the inside of her cheek and fidgets with the end of her sweater sleeve, half expecting her mother to say no.

"Of course, your hair takes to it much better than mine ever has."

My body jumps up and down back at the Station before doing a series of cartwheels and round off back handsprings. She smiles at her daughter, who is a good handful of inches shorter, before leaning down quickly and planting a dry kiss on her forehead.

She turns and hurries down the walkway while Abby steps outside to watch her mother load the beat up Ford Taurus with her meager belongings. She waves a quick goodbye from the driver seat before pulling out into the street. Ten seconds later the back of the car vanishes around a corner. *No hug? And I thought* my *Mom was cold.*

The nippy air causes Abby's arms to break out in goose bumps, so she walks quickly back into the small house, closing the door behind her.

Let's go eat some chocolate.

Abby happily obliges.

Trish Marie Dawson

CHAPTER 20

I remember this feeling like it was yesterday: the lightness in my mind pulling me away, like I'm separating from Abby. I felt this with Sloan too. Only this time I expect it because I'm ready to leave her. For days I simply sit back on my throne and watch as her new world unfolds gloriously around her. The only time I really make an effort for her to hear me is when she makes plans for the following summer out on the lake with Donny and her new friends. I know I will be gone by then. She is slipping away from me more and more each day.

Abby walks to school every day with one of the girls she eats lunch with. She's no longer failing her classes and there's the flat iron of course. The Kardashian sister wannabe's have been downgraded in importance and spend most of their time avoiding Abby as she casually and humbly climbs the social ladder. Donny is exhaustively making his intentions clear: he has it bad for Abby. He walks her to class, follows her around P.E. like a puppy, hands her notes to read in English and yesterday he tucked a rose into her hair at lunch time. It's not just the subtle change in her looks; she's glowing from the inside out and everyone can see it. I now have a bejeweled platinum crown with a matching scepter by my side and Abby's hot P.E. teacher is lying at my feet in a loin cloth fit for the Greek Gods. I lounge in complete euphoria while he hand feeds me red globe grapes. *Oh, the life you can live in someone else's mind.*

Abby is startled awake and I'm pulled away from the to-do list for tomorrow to peer through her sleepy eyes into her dark bedroom. It's almost midnight and some sort of noise has her looking at one of the windows. She shuffles out from under her low-thread count cotton sheets and creeps up to the glass slowly. Why do people always have to look? I half-expect some sort of creature to come flying through the glass and carry her off into the night. Something hard hits the window pane, but doesn't break it. The sound probably isn't loud enough to wake up Abby's grandmother who is asleep down the hall. I think it's some sort of pebble. *Who would be throwing rocks at her window in the middle of the night?*

She carefully peeps through the sheer lace curtains to see a shadowy figure standing below her room, underneath the lower limb of a large shade tree. In the pale moonlight I can see that it's a young man dressed all in black, with a dark cap pulled tightly over his head. *See! Something creepy is waiting just outside the window!* Abby's heart-rate spikes a few beats with fear before she realizes that it's Donny. Uhg. At least it's not something from a Stephen King book - or worse - a girl from school. *What is he doing here…at midnight?!*

Despite my protests, she throws a sweatshirt on and pulls her thin legs into a pair of jeans before dashing down the stairs as quietly as possible. Not that it matters, her grandmother is deaf without her hearing aid on.

Once she reaches the back door, which leads around to the side of the house near the shade tree, she is tugging her feet into a pair of hiking boots. She leaves the laces untied and stumbles her way down the back steps.

Oh, that's safe. Slow down, before you break your neck, silly girl!

When she rounds the corner of the house he is still standing under the tree. I feel a warm and fuzzy feeling ripple through her and tap my missing foot impatiently. *Hurry this up, Abby. You have a math test tomorrow…you need your sleep!*

I feel her take a deep breath, no doubt trying to calm her nerves before she meets him under the red oak. She hugs him hello and watches as he nervously leans against the narrow trunk, twirling the stem of a burgundy leaf between his fingers.

"Hi." Abby says quietly.

"Hi." Donny repeats before smiling shyly.

"You do realize it's the middle of the night, right?" She asks him.

"Oh, I'm sorry." He looks concerned and glances up at the house, before speaking again, "Did I wake you?"

Abby laughs and then clamps her hand over her mouth, looking quickly at the neighbor's house. She moves slightly closer to Donny so that the tree obscures most of her body from the windows next door.

"I just thought, well...do you want to go with me to the Winter Formal together?" Donny says.

"Oh." Abby is surprised and I can tell she is afraid of how to answer.

"If you don't want to, that's okay. It's just a stupid school dance. No worries." Donny adds quickly.

"I do! I mean, of course - that would be nice. It's just..." She trails off with a wave of her hand.

Donny's happy expression falls. "What?"

"What about Ivy and her friends?" Abby looks down at her feet.

I really wish she would raise her head so I could see Donny's face. Instead, he does it for her by reaching forward and using one finger to gently lift her chin, so their faces are inches apart. *That's a much better view.*

"Ivy's not really my type anymore. Plus, she's kind of a jerk." His finger slowly leaves her chin and even in the dark of the night I can see the sparkle in his blue eyes.

Abby's budding feelings for him explode into colorful bloom. She's trying hard not to bounce on her toes.

I told you Abby! He likes you, very much. You just had to give him a try.

Suddenly Donny leans forward again, this time with his mouth and touches his lips gently to Abby's. The kiss is tender and soft and turns Abby's blooming love-flower into an over-flowing garden.

Your first kiss!

When they pull away from each other, Donny's lips turn up into a crooked boyish smile. Abby is glowing, I can feel it. He tucks some of her hair behind her ear and she giggles. *Oh, how I miss the simplicity of first kisses.* As soon as my excitement for her registers, it plummets to the ground. This is exactly how I felt after Ryan Burke kissed me. Suddenly I want nothing more but to get Abby safely inside, behind a closed and locked door.

Wrap this up Abby, time for bed. The fact that she doesn't move tells me she's ignoring me - completely.

"So, will you go with me?" He asks softly.

"Yes."

He kisses her once more before shooing her back into the warm house, to my relief. She rushes through the kitchen and living room and back up the stairs, not bothering to be quiet this time. After returning to her room she pushes the window curtains back to see that he is still under the tree. She waves and he returns the gesture before blowing a kiss up to her window. As he walks away I think he's nothing like Ryan Burke. *Nothing.*

Oh, Abby. How are you ever going to get back to sleep now?

Morning comes too quickly. I didn't do much during the night because Abby was up until well past three and even after she fell asleep she tossed and turned incessantly. If I could yawn I'm sure I would.

Okay, time to start a new day Abby! Let's get up and shower and get ready for school!

I try to ignore the fact that I sound like the mother I never had and follow Abby around her bedroom and bathroom until she is done with her new morning routine. She spends over ten minutes brushing her teeth *just in case* Donny kisses her again today.

On the way to school she tells her new friend Joei all about the night before. Joei is younger but taller than Abby but her voice is child-like and her excited screech is ear-piercing. I don't need my ears around to know they are ringing in protest.

There are two more kisses from Donny before lunch even comes and what I think may be an A on her math test, so it's safe to say that she had a good school day. By the time we are back at home and Abby is sitting down at the small desk made of particle board preparing her homework, I ready myself for what I'm assuming will be an internal struggle. I know that soon I will drift away from her and I don't want it to be before I've had a chance to say everything that needs to be said. I know I won't be called back to the Station early like I was with Sloan but I'm still nervous about leaving any loose ends. Abby will be my first successful case. *I'm sure of it.*

When she is finished with her homework and settles onto her twin bed with a book, I start before I lose my nerve. I think she's ready. I hope she's ready.

Abby...there will be people that hate you for what your father did. But you need to know it's not your fault. Sometimes things go wrong. You need to accept that. You need to know that you will be okay. You're amazing. You can have an amazing life if you choose to live it.

I feel the hot tears start trailing down her cheeks but she doesn't wipe them away. She lets them spill over her jawbone and cascade down the sides of her throat and around to the back of her neck until they pool on the pillow beneath her head.

Abby...you will never be alone. You will find love, friendship and happiness. Believe in yourself Abby, always believe in yourself...

I imagine what I feel later that night as Abby sleeps is like those out of body experiences people talk about. Floating above your body, knowing you are temporarily stuck between the place you knew and what lies beyond and yet feeling at peace. That's what my departure is like. I just sort of glide out of her with this overwhelming sense of harmony and tranquility. It's *beautiful.*

It's not until I feel the connection break completely that I'm aware of my body parts again and the annoying and incredibly uncomfortable pinching sensation starts at my feet and quickly spreads up my body. I brush at my arms, even though I know there is nothing there. It's such a stark contrast to the feeling of peace that I had leaving Abby and immediately I feel drained. I crash back into my reality with so much emotional force that I almost start to cry. It doesn't help that it feels like ants the size of roaches are crawling all over my face. I remember that Niles said some people claim their transition feels like tickling. At this moment I want to find each and every one of those people…and punch them in the nose.

When I arrive back at the Station the first thing I feel is the cool floor under my naked feet and I tuck my toes in, pretending the ground is grass and that my toes are deep inside the moist soil of a Pennsylvania forest. For just a moment I let myself feel sad as I realize it's a sensation I won't ever experience again, at least not in my *own* body. I spend at least a full minute standing in the dark room allowing my imagination to take me to the woods of Erie. I drag my fingers up and down my arms to simulate the feeling of rough tree bark against my skin and imagine that I'm twenty, thirty, forty feet up in the air climbing a giant conifer.

When I open my eyes I see nothing but black. I'm not perched on the top of the highest tree in the woods, or walking barefoot through cool, damp grass. I'm standing in one of the Depot arrival rooms. *Who knew it was possible to miss trees so much?*

I take a deep breath and step forward, knowing that the doorknob will find its way to my palm practically on its own and the moment my warm skin meets the cold metal the door slides effortlessly open. Light floods in around me from the hallway and there to greet me is Niles. I rush into his waiting arms and sigh deeply into his blue sweater vest.

He's patting me on the back and though I can't see his face, I know he's smiling. "I take it this case ended better than the last?"

I nod into his slightly squishy chest. "I did it. I helped her." I beam up at him.

"Yes, dear, you definitely did. How does it feel?" He asks.

"Amazing."

The wrinkles around his eyes deepen as his smile broadens. "That's how it's supposed to feel. If you do it right." He winks at me and points to Abby's card that is in the portal slot I used for Sloan. "Don't forget that."

I cross the room in three strides and pull the slate gray card from the wall. I tenderly hug the thick glass to my chest, this is all that is left of Abby after-all.

We leave the Depot room in happy spirits and enter the long hallway that leads to the other side of the Consignment Department. Niles walks beside me in the hall as we weave around a handful of others. He's listening to the highlights of Abby's case with interest until he notices Carlson bounding towards us with his metal clipboard clutched tightly to his thin chest, as usual.

"Is everything okay, Carlson?" Niles asks him.

"Yes, yes. But I need to speak with you Abbot," he pauses to clear his throat and sends a nervous glance in my direction. *I just got back, surely I couldn't have done something wrong, could I?* "It's um, it's about her."

"Piper?" Niles seems just as surprised as me. *I have done something.*

Carlson bobs his head up and down and looks at me again with an almost pained expression on his face. *Wow, this must be bad.*

"I'll be right back, Piper. Okay?" Niles tries to smile at me, but it doesn't do much good. I can't speak so I just nod my head and watch them walk down the hall together, disappearing into one of the small rooms. *Oh crap. What's happened now?!*

I stand awkwardly in the hallway holding Abby's glass card to my chest like it's a life raft. I feel like I'm floating alone in the sea and every time someone walks past me and bumps into my arm or shoulder the sensation startles my body and my insides rise up and down, like waves from an ocean storm.

I'm pretty sure I've made myself sea-sick by the time Niles and Carlson exit the small room and I almost puke on my feet when I see that his face is set into a worried frown. I've spent however long it was that he was in the next room running through everything I did with Abby. I followed ALL the rules, more so with her than I did with Sloan. I'm confident that I haven't done anything too awful to involve Niles. *So what's going on?!*

"Piper." He says my name softly.

I nod, waiting for my banishment or public humiliation to come. Niles simply takes my hand and pulls me next to him. We begin walking back down the hall, toward the room he and Carlson spoke in and suddenly I panic.

"No, wait."

I stop hard enough that the soles of my bare-feet squeak loudly as they skid on the smooth, cold surface of the Consignment Department floor. Niles stares at me, waiting for an explanation.

"Who's in there? Am I in trouble?" My voice is strained to a point that even I don't recognize it.

"It's nothing like that, dear. But I need you to come with me. Please?" He holds his hand out and I count slowly to ten before placing my fingers onto his outstretched palm. Forget shaky hands, my entire body is trembling. I've just begun to follow him when Carlson rushes at us, muttering.

"Crap. Crap." Carlson nearly drops his clipboard at his feet as he attempts to hurry down the hall.

Niles glances over my shoulder to follow Carlson's gaze and freezes in place, his mouth agape, his hand gripped tightly around mine.

"Niles? Are you okay?" I ask, afraid of the shocked look on his face. Slowly I tug my fingers from his grasp and shift slightly as Niles continues to stare at something behind me.

Suddenly I bump shoulders with a taller man as he rushes by my left side and I'm spun in a half circle by the force. I hear him mutter an apology just as he passes me but his attention is set on Carlson.

Niles is staring at the man, a look of concern on his face before he glimpses down at me briefly. I glance back in Carlson's direction, not understanding at all what is happening. He's now talking to the tall man that collided with me in the busy hallway. I see nothing extraordinary about him, other than the fact that he must be a New Arrival since he's holding the single sheet of Station Guidelines from Orientation carefully in one hand. His six-foot build towers over the fragile looking Carlson but he still seems small in the hallway After Carlson speaks to him, the tall man straightens and begins scanning the busy hallway looking for someone. He raises a toned arm up to push his hair off his forehead as he turns in my direction and I catch a peek of something green beneath the sleeve of his t-shirt.

My entire body goes weak and my fingers release their tight hold on Abby's card as our eyes meet. The glass slides down the front of my baggy shirt and hits the hard floor with a sickening sound as it shatters loudly around my feet. I don't notice it. But everyone else does, including Niles, who gasps beside me. All eyes turn to face me; the girl that just destroyed a precious and irreplaceable Assignment Card, but I focus only on the man standing ten feet away.

Carlson gapes at me in horror. He clutches his metal clipboard to his chest and shakes his head disapprovingly at me. But I'm not looking at him. I can't tear my eyes away from the shocked man by his side. Carlson quickly grumbles something to the New Arrival. I watch as he leans down to hear what Carlson has to say and a familiar set of dark curls drop over his forehead. *No, no, no, NO, NO!*

Everyone is still staring at me. Niles is kneeling on the ground, sweeping some of the glass shards into his hand but I don't care. I don't care that Abby's case is lost forever, because *he* is here.
Sloan is at the Station.

The End of Book 1

ACKNOWLEDGEMENTS

Before I begin to thank the people that helped make this book possible, I'd like to take a moment to bring up the subject matter in this story that may have been intense for some readers. To start, I'd like to say that this book is not meant to glorify suicide in *any way*. If you or someone you know is having suicidal thoughts, please contact your health care professional or another person you trust to talk to TODAY. If you are considering harming yourself in *any way*, there are people and professionals that can help you. You are not alone. Ever.

If you or someone you know has been the victim of sexual violence, you can find help here on http://www.rainn.org/or you can call the National Sexual Assault Hotline at 1-800-656-HOPE. Again, you are not alone.

This book would not have been possible without the ongoing support of family and friends. So now I'd like to take the time to thank you all personally!

Shane, Rory and Foxx - you give me encouragement and hope. This book, the one before and anything in the future would not be possible without your daily support and love. Thank you for being patient and for the hugs.

To my extended family: Mom, I love you, I am who I am because of you. Thank you for everything! Teresa...you aren't here today but I hope wherever you are, you know how much you have meant to me over the years and how much you meant to me while I was writing this book. You were my personal cheerleader and I miss you every day. I'll never forget your laugh. Mom, Aunts, Uncles and Cousins - last year was a tough one for all of us but we made it through - love you all. Grandma Dawson, you are an amazing woman. I love you and I hope I've made you proud. To my wonderful in-laws - Rick and Lynda…Shane and I would not be where we are today without your ongoing support and love, thank you.

To my good friends: Debbie Rogers, Irene Aranda, Kerry Bigelow, Steph Perry-Aguirre, Hector Aguirre, Gladys Selfridge, Sean Selfridge, Jennifer Peterson, Patty Calles, Jessica Garner and Melinda Lenard…I love you all equally, thank you for your friendship and for listening to my writing rants and raves.

Thank you to my Editing Team: Jennifer Peterson and Tracy Clark - thank you so much for your help and dedication!

The Cover Art for this book was done by the amazing Debbie Rogers - thank you friend!

Thank you Book Club ladies for keeping me reading even though I'm busy writing! A thank you has to go out to my new friends on Facebook & Twitter. You all KNOW who you are but I have to give a special shout out to the ladies that make me laugh…*every day*. My fellow writer friends: Miranda Stork, Karli Rush and Tara Wood. The Man Candy has kept me going. Truth.

For the very special people who have read this book and might have read the first one - THANK YOU ALL. This is for you guys. HUGS!

.

ABOUT THE AUTHOR

Trish was born and mostly raised in San Diego, California where she lives now with her family and pets. She's been writing short stories and poetry since high school and began her first book, 'I Hope You Find Me' in December of 2011.

When Trish isn't writing, she's homeschooling her amazing daughter and mildly Autistic son, reading whatever she can get her hands on, or enjoying the Southern California sun. As a strict Vegetarian, Trish holds a special place in her heart for animal rights and dashes into the backyard weekly to rescue lizards and mice from Zoey, the dog.

TRISH'S BOOKS & COLLABORATIONS:

<u>FIND ME</u> Series
I Hope You Find Me
Lost & Found (Coming Soon)

<u>THE STATION</u> Series
Dying to Forget
Dying to Remember
Dying to Return (Coming Soon)

<u>ANTHOLOGIES</u>
Via Moon Rose Publishing:
Once Upon A Twisted Time (Hawke & the Beast)

You Can Follow Trish Here:

Twitter
https://twitter.com/Trish_Dawson

Facebook
https://www.facebook.com/WriterTrishMarieDawson

Trish's Blog
http://writertrishmdawson.wordpress.com

Trish's eBooks can be found online on Amazon as well as in print. Please support your favorite Indie Author's by buying their books and leaving them honest reviews.

Say NO to book piracy!

Pretty Little Weeds
PUBLISHING